Pieces of

BROKEN TIME

By

Lorenz Font

Books by Lorenz Font

The Gates Legacy Series

Hunted - Book 1

Tormented - Book 2

Ascension - Book 3

Reckoning - Book 4

Redemption - Book 5 – Coming soon

Indivisible Line

Feather Light

Pieces of Broken Time

The Prodian Journey Series

Rise of Alpha

Pieces of Broken Time

By
Lorenz Font

Talem
Publication

Cover Images: Ginasanders/dreamstime John Pilge/sxu.hu
Cover Design: Claudia Trapp/Phantasy Graphic Design
www.phantasygraphicdesign.com

Interior Design - Jennifer McGuire | JEMBookDesigns.com

http://www.lorenzfont.com

To Doug Nelson,
A friend, gentleman, and guardian angel.
You will never be forgotten.

July 10, 2000

"Bro, you good?" Trent Shaw's voice broke into Blake Connor's thoughts, distracting him from the hypnotic drone of the plane's whirring engine.

Blinking his eyes, Blake nodded and patted his best friend on the back. "Yeah. It's all good."

En route to Nigeria for an extensive training mission, they faced endless hours of hard work and planning as members of the Special Forces. Briefing had taken less than a week and while the exact purpose and length of their service in the region was still being debated in Washington, Blake was eager to get his first real assignment underway. Training was a different mindset. He'd been jonesing for the real deal.

Alongside Blake sat a fellow Californian, Trent, with sharp green eyes and an easy smile, as well as two rednecks, Robert and Shane. The excitement inside the cabin was palpable.

Robert blew a big gum bubble and made a loud, annoying sound as he popped it back in his mouth. "I hope this stint finishes in time for the baby."

"I'm crossing my fingers for ya, buddy," Shane said.

Blake grinned as the rest of the guys muttered their agreement and saluted Robert.

Fatherhood was a blessing but not something Blake was ready for. In fact, he doubted he'd ever commit until he was out of the military. Going off on assignments for an unknown period of time and leaving a family behind should be avoided, in his book. Remaining unattached was the only way to go.

With a thirty minute estimated time of arrival, Blake felt the plane drop altitude. His heart skipped a beat and he glanced at Trent. His best friend for the past year was completely lost in the photograph he held in the palm of his hand. Without even seeing it, Blake knew it was a picture of Trent's girlfriend, Jennifer Owens.

He elbowed Trent. "You're going to burn a hole in that picture if you don't stop staring at it."

"Be that as it may, I miss the lady already," Trent said and lowered his lips to the picture, giving it a loud kiss.

"Dude, we've only been gone for eleven hours. You gotta be kidding me." Blake shook his head.

"You're such a lech, Shaw." Joe, another Ranger from Texas, teased Trent.

Rolling his eyes, Trent gave the picture another kiss before placing it in his pocket. "I'm just keeping it real."

The pilot's voice crackled over the speaker to announce their arrival at the small military airstrip.

The plane continued its descent, and Blake readied for action.

Deep down, he envied his friends. Blake's decision to remain single had nothing to do with not finding the right girl but with wanting one that wasn't available. Although Katrina had been more than willing almost from the start, Blake hadn't been able to bring himself to commit, and it wasn't fair to string Katrina along when she wasn't the woman invading his every waking thought.

Blake shoved his beret off and ran his hand over his skull trim, inhaling a deep breath. With a final glance at Trent's pocket, Blake exhaled slowly and admitted, even if it was only to himself, that this whole thing was a nightmare waiting to happen.

Colonel Norwalk stood up once the aircraft settled to a stop, and removed an unlit cigarillo from his mouth. "You kids ready to roll?"

A collective and enthusiastic response echoed from all the rangers present, and they exited the plane like an ant colony ready for a hard day's labor.

—◦◦◦—

"Hey, baby. Is everything okay?"

Blake heard Trent whispering into the phone on one of their rare work breaks. A long pause followed and he assumed his buddy was listening to his fiancée on the other end. Blake tried to move away to avoid hearing any more of the conversation. He'd rather not be in the same room but the cramped space didn't allow for much movement. He turned his back and picked up a local newspaper as a distraction.

As much as he'd been able, Blake had been keeping his feelings on a tight leash concerning the woman he'd been thinking of, which had been difficult since all the eavesdropping had made him privy to the rough patch that Jennifer was going through back home.

When he read the same sentence for a fourth time and still had no idea what it said, he knew he was choking on his feelings and losing all ability to concentrate.

Trent covered the mouthpiece and summoned him over. "Blake, come say hi to Jennifer and cheer her up?"

Hesitating, he had no idea how to get out of this one. He looked around the confined space as if the answer was hiding in a corner. It was too late to make a halfhearted excuse, so he took a deep breath and worked at modulating his voice to sound upbeat before he took the phone from Trent. "Hey, Jenny, how is our up and coming clothing designer?" *Good enough.* His tone came out sounding bright and cheery. *Brownie point for me.*

Despite the dark clouds he knew loomed around her aunt's health woes, Jennifer's giggle surprised him and caused a strange sensation to ripple across his taut nerves.

"I'm fine. How are you doing? Loving the weather so far?"

"Sure. Showers are required three times a day in this oppressive oven." He chuckled. Damn him for allowing himself to relish the sweet lilt of her voice. He cleared his throat and tried to settle himself. "Is your aunt going to be okay?"

There was a pause on the other end.

Blake could only imagine the difficulty of the situation, considering their wedding was scheduled soon.

"I don't know exactly what to think anymore. It's scary."

Trying to sound optimistic for her benefit, Blake said, "Well, better get Aunt Debbie up and about. You don't want to miss the rare sight of me in a tuxedo."

Another edgy laugh sounded on the other end of the line.

Blake couldn't stop the feeling of helplessness that hit him square in the chest. Helpless for wanting someone he could never have. He threw a quick glance at Trent, who was gnawing his finger out of nervous habit.

"I'm crossing my fingers." Jennifer sounded wistful, which only made Blake ache for her more than ever.

"Well, I have to go now. We're on a tight schedule here. Take care of yourself, ya hear?" It was a fib, but the longer he stayed on the phone, the more trouble he made for himself.

"You men behave yourselves," she said.

"Yes, ma'am. We're all vying for sainthood here." Blake handed the phone back to Trent and stepped back. He flipped through the newspaper in an effort to keep his mind off replaying the sound of her voice in his head, and not wanting to hear the sad goodbyes or silly I love yous.

After the phone call that seemed to last forever, he and Trent walked out of the designated communication station and into the blistering heat. The night temperature hadn't improved, and it left them sweating underneath their brown shirts and camouflage pants.

"What's the deal with her aunt?" Blake asked. He knew what had prompted the unscheduled call from Jennifer and sent Trent into a spiral of worry.

"Aunt Debbie is not doing well. She refuses to be admitted to the hospital, and Jennifer is running out of hope."

"That blows. What about the wedding?"

"I don't know." Sadness crept into Trent's voice. "I wish I could be there to help out."

Blake had nothing more for his friend apart from a pat on the shoulder for comfort.

They reached their barracks and slipped quietly through the dark, as lights out was already in force.

"I hope she gets better so she can give Jennifer away. It would break her heart if her aunt couldn't attend the wedding," Trent whispered before they each climbed into their own makeshift cots.

The next few days stretched into a blur of activities while the mission took form. In spite of the busy schedule, Blake spent each day vacillating between beating himself up for every thought of Jennifer and attempting to divert his full attention to Katrina. The task had proven difficult. His mind kept wandering to the beautiful, petite blonde with expressive eyes. While he had spoken to her countless times, he'd only seen her once, but it had been enough. He had known the moment he'd seen her smile that he was in trouble.

August 15, 2001

After the short gig in Nigeria, followed by a reassignment in Sierra Leone, Blake returned to the States expecting to finish off the rest of the summer awaiting his next deployment. A brief lull from working and travelling called for a little rest. Relaxing was a well-deserved change of pace. He welcomed the comfort of sleeping in his own bed and looked forward to the time where he and Drew, a Doberman puppy he'd recently bought, could spend time in the park playing ball and taking long walks.

With keys in hand and Drew in tow, they were ready to sail out the door when the phone rang. The strong urge to ignore the call was replaced with worry. His parents were the only ones who called his landline.

"Hello?" he said, gesturing for Drew to heel.

"Hey, my man, Jennifer and I are in town, and we have to hang out." Trent sounded too enthusiastic.

"In town?" Blake glanced at the wall clock and swallowed his groan. "When? Where?" He wasn't ready to see Jennifer again. No matter how nice she was or how hard he'd tried to keep his feelings hidden, he might slip and that would be a shitload of trouble.

"Yeah, we're in a hotel in Westwood right now. Why don't you drive here and we'll meet you at the bar?"

Crap! This can't be happening.

"Um, okay. I'll be there around seven tonight." He wrote down the name of the hotel and hung up feeling as if he were about to attend his own funeral. His plan had been to avoid Jennifer until the wedding.

It seemed the mighty guy up there had other plans for him.

Jennifer stared at Trent in disbelief. "Are you sure about this?"

"I don't want us to get married while Aunt Debbie is the way she is right now. I'm glad she finally relented to be taken to the hospital, though. I think it's a good idea if we postpone the wedding until she's feeling better and up on her feet." Trent took her hand and kissed it.

"I feel terrible." She tilted his chin until his green eyes were gazing into hers.

"Rubbish." Trent smiled, a slow and easy one, and she knew he understood. "Besides, what is another month? You will be Mrs. Shaw in no time."

Aunt Debbie had been suffering shortness of breath, and the last stroke had snuffed every ounce of energy from them both. Jennifer had felt bad preparing for her wedding while her aunt's health had been on a downward spiral, but she couldn't help the sense of relief she'd felt with Trent's announcement. He'd understood, and her guilt was killing her. She shouldn't want to celebrate postponing their wedding. She knew the answer but cowardice made her ignore the facts staring her in the face.

The wedding would take place in a month. There hadn't been too many arrangements since she had made it clear that she wanted a small ceremony in front of a judge and attended by only a few family and friends, with a reception at a local restaurant afterward. She suspected that Trent was more interested in the honeymoon anyway.

At Aunt Debbie's insistence, Jennifer had agreed to let her move into a nursing facility close to home with twenty-four-hour health care professionals, even though she had hated her aunt's decision. Jennifer had no doubt that it had to do with Trent's arrival, but she'd had no choice but to follow the dear woman's wishes. Caring for her only relative wasn't a task. How could it be when her aunt had given up so much? It was the least she could do for the woman who had taken her in as her own after her parents had perished in an automobile accident.

"Why don't we go to Los Angeles and take in the sights? We can stay a couple of nights and maybe call Blake for a drink, too."

Trent's suggestion sounded appealing, and the mini vacation allowed her to get away while still being close enough in case Aunt Debbie needed her. It could be nice seeing Blake again, too.

Just nice?

Jennifer had taken an instant liking to Trent's best friend, Blake. He was easygoing, funny, and genuine. Trent was an only child, but the day they started training he had immediately adopted the man with the similar twisted sense of humor as his brother. During their deployment together, Trent had talked nonstop about his friend and Jennifer felt as though she'd known the guy practically her whole life.

Jennifer chewed her bottom lip a moment longer before she pushed the smile into place. "Sure, let me just call the hospital. Let them know that I'll be away for the weekend."

Packed inside Trent's SUV and headed toward Los Angeles, Jennifer enjoyed the scenery and a few moments of comfortable silence when she noticed Trent furrowing his brows.

"Penny for your thoughts?"

"Hmm?" Trent glanced at her and smiled, reaching across the console to hold her hand. "I'm just thinking of the future. Life in general."

"What about it?"

He only hesitated a second before answering, but it was enough that she caught it. "I don't know. I'm just full of introspection these days."

"Are you getting cold feet?" She had no idea what had prompted her to ask. Trent's reluctance to look her in the eye told her that she might be on to something. She expected to feel guilt for asking, but it was relief that washed over her. Embarrassed at her internal jubilation, she stared straight ahead.

Trent grinned. "Oh no. It's not that. I'm just being silly." He touched her chin briefly before focusing on the road again.

"You know you can tell me anything."

Trent smiled. "You know I love you, right? And I'll try to do right by you."

Jennifer nodded. "And I love you, too." She leaned over and kissed his cheek, hoping to find the nerve to admit that she wasn't sure about anything anymore. As usual, she couldn't say it. The last thing she wanted to do was to hurt Trent.

The background music substituted for the lack of conversation, and Jennifer closed her eyes while the calming melody lulled her to the special place where she rarely allowed herself to go—the day of her engagement party.

"May I have this dance?"

Blake's voice sounded so close, prompting Jennifer to open her eyes and glance at the man beside her before she was lost in her memories once more.

Pride had radiated in Trent's face when he'd kissed her hand and stepped aside, placing her hand in Blake's. "Take care of her. She is a treasure."

"As she is to me."

Blake's voice was barely audible, but she heard it. Her heart raced, making her weak in the knees. She expected to feel this way in her fiancé's presence, not with Blake.

"Excuse me?" she asked.

Blake inclined his head and flashed a stunning smile. "Shall we?" he said, ignoring her inquiry. Without waiting for an answer, he spun her around and then placed a hand on the small of her back, swaying to the rhythm of the slow music.

"What did you just say a minute ago?" Feeling a bit breathless, she let him guide her around the dance floor, basking in the strength of his touch. It felt wrong, and yet so right.

"Trent is lucky to have you."

"What do you mean?" Her hands grew clammy from the mere touch of this man holding her.

"I wish I had someone like you," he whispered.

Jennifer closed her eyes for a brief moment, unable to utter a coherent reply. This man was wreaking havoc inside her. She moved a fraction, creating a little distance between their bodies, but Blake pulled her back to him. When she opened her eyes, she found him staring at her while they continued to dance. The dizzying sensation made it impossible to think.

"I have no doubt that you'll find the perfect woman for you," she finally said.

"I'm staring at perfection right now." There was a trace of melancholy in his voice that made her ache to probe deeper into his soul.

She had rested her cheek against his chest to avoid looking at him. It had been best to disregard his words and pretend she hadn't heard him.

It was no surprise that Trent's first order of business after getting checked into the hotel was calling Blake.

With details arranged and confirmed, Jennifer decided to take a long, luxurious bath complete with bubbles, a glass of champagne, and a book.

She hadn't been lounging long when Trent knocked and peeked around the edge of the door. "Can I join you?" he asked.

Jennifer grinned and slid up in the tub, making room for him. "Sure."

Trent settled behind her, cradling her body between his legs.

"Comfortable?" she asked.

"I always am when you're around," he whispered into her hair.

Jennifer settled against his chest and let the rise and fall of his breathing lull her.

He's here, but—no time like the present.

Jennifer took a deep breath and tried to swallow around the lump in her throat. "Is something wrong? I feel like there's something going on . . .

something you're not telling me." She tilted her head just in time to catch Trent clenching his jaw—a sure sign she was on the right path with her question.

Trent kept tracing the contour of her body with his fingers as he seemed to work through exactly how much he wanted to say. "In the event of my death, I've asked Blake to watch over you until you find someone who can make you happy."

Water splashed over the edge of the tub when she whirled to face him. "What are you talking about? Nothing's going to happen to you. Do you hear what I'm saying?"

"There is nothing set in this life, my sweet."

His quiet, matter-of-fact tone sent shivers up her spine. "You're not going anywhere. You want two babies, right? Well, they need a father growing up."

Another painful expression shot across his face.

Jennifer sensed the battle raging within him.

Kids was a conversation they hadn't had in several weeks, but having both come from one-child households, they had agreed that two was the perfect number. The children got the best of everything and all without spreading her and Trent too thin.

He blinked once.

Is-is he crying?

His voice croaked when he responded. "Yeah, two is a manageable number."

"Is there anything you haven't told me?" Dread washed over her, sapping the warmth from the tub water, and pulled another full body shiver out of her.

Trent closed his eyes for a brief moment, and when he opened them, he offered a weak smile. He shook his head. "I love you, Jennifer."

"I love you, too." With all the tenderness she possessed, now coupled with a fear of the unknown and the terror of losing another loved one, Jennifer seized his lips and kissed him.

Trent returned her kisses with equal amounts of passion and alacrity, and by the time they surfaced for air, she felt his hard-on poking her stomach.

Jennifer let her hand glide down to his hardened shaft.

Trent stiffened and held her at arm's length. "We better get ready. Blake should be here in an hour, and we still have to grab dinner."

His blatant refusal felt like a slap in the face, but Jennifer was too stunned to form a coherent reply. Had she done or said anything wrong? Was Trent finally realizing that it was a mistake to ask her to marry him?

"Baby, did you hear me? Would you like to dine downstairs or just order in?"

Tears stung her eyes and she choked back the lump in her throat. "Um, in—let's order in," she answered.

Dinner arrived and no matter how she tried to enjoy the mouth-watering fare he'd ordered, everything tasted like cardboard. She mustered a brave face on his behalf. Trent was only around for a few weeks, a month at most, and she hated to spend it fighting.

Afterward, they made their way down in the elevator and into the pulsating bar with a techno beat pounding from the speakers.

Trent wove his arm protectively around her waist as they snaked through the throngs of people walking and dancing on the small dance floor.

Jennifer glanced at Trent and, while dread still weighed heavy in her mind, she felt his body relax and watched his face light up like a Christmas tree upon spotting Blake at the bar, waving.

Even from afar, Blake was alarmingly handsome, just as she remembered him. His easy smile greeted them as they approached.

"Jennifer," Blake said, and gave her a quick peck on the cheek. "Here, take this seat." He took her elbow and guided her to the barstool. "Good to see you."

"Blake, how have you been?" Her voice fared better than his formal greeting. It made her wonder if the detached demeanor was only meant for her. *Don't take it personal. Just breathe, Jennifer!*

"It's not often that my best friend and his fiancée are in town, so allow me to get you both drunk and happy. We're taking shots!" Blake summoned the lady bartender, who took his order while devouring him with her eyes.

Amused, Jennifer studied a side of Blake she hadn't seen before. The pictures Trent had sent her hadn't done Blake justice. In person, he was bigger than life. A smile always lit his face, and his eyes were the most mesmerizing blue she'd ever seen. His rugged charm had several women doing a double take, and Jennifer was certain she almost heard a couple of them purring. Add Trent to the mix, and the two of them were too much for the female population of the room, who stumbled over their own two feet trying to get a closer look at the gorgeous men. Deep down, she sensed that there was more to Blake than just striking good looks. He seemed in tune with his emotions and sensitive to others' feelings as well.

Jennifer couldn't believe how oblivious the guys were to the stir they created around them, and the main attractions at the bar were focused completely on her. Their easy banter back and forth was just loud enough to make her part of their teasing, despite the loud music in the background.

The moment their drinks came, Blake raised his shot glass. "For my best bud and his girl, may life treat you with kindness. Here's to many, *many* years of happiness together."

"Thanks, my man," Trent said and took her hand, giving it a squeeze.

They bumped glasses and downed the clear liquid in one quick gulp.

While Jennifer struggled with the burning effect of the tequila, Blake waved his hand again at the bartender. "Give us another round."

"So any ideas where we're headed next?" Trent asked.

"Can't we just talk about something else? I'm hoping to catch some decent waves while I'm here," Blake said.

Jennifer watched the two men talk animatedly while they launched into recollections of past deployments and comical conversations among the other Army Rangers. Trent seemed to relax even more as the night progressed, but she still saw the strain in his eyes every time he glanced at her.

If Blake noticed, he didn't say anything. He kept everyone entertained with bottomless drinks and easy chatter.

She caught him sneaking a glance in her direction several times during the course of the night, but he didn't make her uncomfortable. On the contrary, he was much too jolly for her taste, as if he was trying hard to appear upbeat.

Trent was lucky to have such a good friend in Blake. Jennifer recognized the same easy relationship with her best friend, Coleen Newhart. If she could find someone good enough for the man with the easygoing personality and arresting charm, she wouldn't mind playing cupid. She just knew he would be a great catch.

It was well past one in the morning by the time Trent announced that he'd had enough. Jennifer had stopped hours ago, at shot number five.

"I'm ready to crash." Trent could barely lift his head as he skimmed his lips along her neck.

"I better get a room," Blake said. "I don't think a DUI would be good to have in my record."

"Bullshit, man. Crash in our room. We have a suite. You can take the couch. Just do not fuckin' snore, okay?" Trent landed a playful slap on Blake's shoulder.

Jennifer decided to jump in. "Yeah, stay in our suite. Just don't snore. I'm not equipped for a duet."

Blake hesitated for a moment before he nodded and chuckled. "I can't promise anything, my dear."

Jennifer climbed off the barstool and linked arms with each of the men, and they made their way toward the elevator, weaving like the crazy drunks that they were.

September 25, 2001

"Drew. Sit, boy." Blake nudged the Doberman aside with his knee while he carried groceries from the garage into the kitchen. The big oaf could smell pig ears a mile away.

The dog sat on his haunches with his eyes fixed on the bag that Blake set down on the counter.

"Good boy." He rummaged inside the paper sack, watching Drew wag his tail so hard the dog's whole body shook. Blake pulled out the bag containing the treats, took one out, and held it up.

Drew watched him with focused interest while Blake walked toward the sliding glass door and slid it open.

His rented townhouse in a suburb a few miles from LA had a little concrete slab for a patio, but it was enough space that the dog could spend most of his time outside rather than cooped up in the house. The warm, midsummer breeze wafted in as Blake strode out, wiggling the treat in the air.

Drew perked his cropped ears but he never moved, his eyes glued to Blake's hand. When Blake threw the pig ear across the yard, the dog watched it fly through the air yet remained in his spot. He glanced up at Blake, his sleek body vibrating with expectation, and waited for his command.

"Go!"

Drew sailed off the patio and into the yard.

Blake chuckled and returned to the kitchen, put the groceries away, and started lunch. After retrieving his mac and cheese from the microwave, he sat at his dinette and rummaged through his mail. He grinned at the newest edition of *Playboy* and set it aside, planning to read it cover to cover at bedtime. Forking a big bite of macaroni into his mouth, he pulled out a bill from the gas company, a credit card statement, and a car payment notice. Blake glanced through the rest of the junk mail until he spotted the familiar Army postmark.

He straightened in his chair, and a strange emotion washed over him as he stared at the envelope. It was lightweight, but something told him this wasn't one of those one-page announcements they sent out from time to time. Since he'd just returned from Sierra Leone a few months ago, he'd hoped for more down time before the next assignment.

He ripped the envelope open, unfolded the paper, and began to read. Skimming past the greetings, he located the crux of the letter—"*report to your superior at Fort Benning in one week.*" There were no other instructions given.

Blake stared at the letter until his vision began to blur, while possible scenarios raced through his head. With the recent attacks on US soil by a group of Islamic militants, he'd sort of expected this. Given the heinous nature of the crime, he had figured it would be a matter of time before the government would take military action. He might be jumping the gun, but his gut told him where his next destination would be.

Eventually Blake stood and, with automatic motions, tossed what was left of his lunch, washed his fork and glass, called Drew back inside, and then moved upstairs.

First things first.

It wasn't a phone call he wanted to make, but he had no choice.

Blake dialed his parents' number, and his mother picked up on the first ring.

"Hello?"

"Mom? Is Dad there with you?" Better if they heard his announcement together, in case they asked questions, which he was certain that they would.

"He's here. Jack . . . Blake's on the phone! Take the cordless in the kitchen."

"Blake, what's going on?" his father asked.

"Mom, Pops . . ." Blake took a long, deep breath before exhaling the lungful of air. "I'm leaving in a week. Destination unknown."

Several long seconds of silence ticked by then his mother gasped, and a sob tore through the phone line.

He heard his father clear his throat. "Blake, you're good, right?"

"Yes, Pops. I'm tight."

His father didn't ask any other questions. Jack Connor was a man of few words who stuck with relevant information and what he deemed important to Blake. Goodbyes had never been one of those things.

"Is there anything you want me to do for you, son?"

"There is something I'm hoping you can do."

"Say the word."

"Can you take Drew in while I'm away? I hate to take him to the kennel since I have no idea how long I'll be gone—"

"You got it. Anything else?" That was Jack, direct and no-nonsense. Blake had always liked that about his father.

"Can I leave my Jeep with you, too?"

"I'll be happy to drive the gas guzzler for you."

Even though Jack's attempt to lighten up the conversation worked, Blake still felt the unspoken tension. The sooner he got off the phone, the better it'd be for all of them.

"Blake." His mother tried to keep her voice even. "Write and call us whenever you can?"

"Yes, Mom. I promise I will. Every chance I get." He hung up before the waterworks began.

Blake dialed Katrina's number. He drummed his fingers on his nightstand, waiting for her to answer. When her voice mail picked up, he hung up.

There were no expectations between him and Katrina. Their relationship was easy—too easy sometimes—and they acted more like fuck-buddies than lovers, calling when either one of them needed a release. Still, he'd rather tell her this kind of news in person than leave it on a message.

He gathered his keys from the hallway bureau and patted Drew's head before he walked to the garage.

Dissecting their relationship was difficult. Though he and Katrina had dated off and on in college, they'd kept things light and had remained friends. They'd kept in contact with each other even after graduation. Katrina had branched off into real estate not long after she had earned her accounting degree. Dainty and with the most gorgeous blue eyes he'd ever seen, Katrina was feisty and just what Blake had needed in his life.

It took twenty minutes to reach her beach house in the affluent suburb of Manhattan Beach, steps away from the ocean.

When she opened the door, Blake knew his announcement could wait. There was a more pressing matter he'd rather attend to first.

"Hey, Blake," she said in her usual sweet tone. She looked almost regal with her blond hair arranged in an intricate and elegant twist at the top of her head.

He let his eyes rake over her full, inviting lips and down to the V of her robe, where her rounded cleavage peeked out. He licked his lips in anticipation while crossing the threshold and claimed her mouth.

An hour and several orgasms later, they rested and listened to each other's ragged breaths, smiling at yet another satisfying time together.

Blake propped on the arm of the sofa. "I got a letter in the mail today." He didn't have to say any more. Katrina was all too familiar with the nature of his career.

Her relaxed and laid-back demeanor turned into one of indifference. "So this is it, huh?"

"I guess. I don't know how long it'll take before I get back. I don't want you to wait." Blake watched her grimace.

"Sure, but call me if you get the chance. I still want to know what's going on with you." She stood up, not bothering to cover her body.

Blake eyed her naked figure as she walked toward the bathroom and shut the door behind her. He couldn't help but notice she returned with a lit cigarette in one hand and an ashtray in the other.

Katrina rarely smoked, only indulging in the vice when she was stressed or nervous.

"I will, but no promises. We agreed on this." Blake picked up his jeans and shirt from the floor and got dressed.

"Yes, we did." Katrina blew out a cloud of smoke and smiled. "Take good care of yourself, Blake."

Ignoring the fact that the smile had never reached her eyes, he leaned forward and tousled her hair. "You, too. Take care of yourself." He left without looking back.

He hadn't missed the soft sob that followed the click of the door any more than he had the cigarette, but he refused to dwell on it. He had a week to pack, move his belongings out of his rented townhouse, and get Drew situated. He didn't have time for bad habits or sure signs of things to come.

October 19, 2001 ~ Kandahar, Afghanistan

Briefing had lasted a week. Right after Blake's unit was given their specific tasks, they shipped out of Fort Benning for a fifteen-hour flight to the southern part of Afghanistan. Once again, Blake and Trent's assignments had reunited them.

The two had first met and struck up an odd friendship during basic training. They had both volunteered as Ranger candidates. Their constant jokes and ribbing had helped them survive MOS, jump school, and RIP together. At this point, it was more than a relief to share the same duty again.

The Army Rangers, together with other special operations forces, were set to spearhead ground operations and conduct air assaults on several sites in response to 9/11 and the attacks on US soil. Their aircraft was equipped to drop a couple of hundred soldiers on a landing strip near Kandahar, Blake and Trent among them.

The air was hot and thick with dust as they secured the area. Blake moved with efficiency, following orders and taking Trent's left flank. With his pulse thumping in his ears, Blake felt the rush of adrenaline pumping in his body when they worked with seamless accuracy with the rest of the unit, stabilizing the landing zone with minimal resistance. The entire seize and secure objective had lasted six hours with only a few minor injuries sustained by their unit.

Blake and Trent chose the barracks closest to the radios at base camp.

Blake lay with his head propped on his arms, one foot twitching back and forth, and staring into the dark at the makeshift ceiling.

"Can't sleep?" Trent asked, as he shifted and tossed on his cot, sighing loudly, and making enough noise to keep everyone awake.

Shane pounded on the wall. "Stop it, Shaw!"

Several of the other guys started a chorus of groaning and complaining.

"With you bouncing around like an elephant on a squeaky spring, I doubt I'll ever be able to sleep." Blake grunted in the darkness as he punched the flat lump posing as a pillow underneath him.

Although their quarters quieted down right away, the echoes of gunshots replayed in Blake's head like a broken record. As foolish as it sounded, he relished the action of a firefight. The adrenaline rush temporarily made him forget his homesickness. Besides, who could sleep in the numbing cold after the oppressive heat of the day? Add in the dust, which was as thick as clouds, and it felt like he was going to be sick.

And to think that it was just his first day back.

Trent snorted. "I'm sure it's someone you left back home that's keeping you awake. Is it that pretty gal you're screwing?"

Yeah, right.

If he was being honest with himself, he knew he had just been stringing her along—an easy lay without the promise of anything concrete. "Sorry, bro, you got the wrong guy. I believe *you're* the one who's having separation anxiety, man. By the way, how's Jennifer?"

Chuckling, Trent told him more stories about his fiancée with animated excitement.

While the rest of the guys fell into deep slumber, the pair continued talking until the wee hours of the morning. Blake learned how Jennifer had been dealing with her aunt's deteriorating health while juggling her career, and as Trent continued talking about her, Blake couldn't shake the vision of her lovely face from his mind. The woman his friend spoke of with such profound admiration and affection left him wanting to know more about her, and their meeting had given him a glimpse of exactly what he wanted in a woman. Trent was a lucky bastard for landing a great catch.

Mesmerized by their love story, Blake had found it difficult not to feel envy and wish he had a woman awaiting his return and keeping their bed warm in his absence. It was a long shot considering his relationship with Katrina which, although easy and relaxed, had no depth to it. It was missing the most important aspect—he wasn't in love with Katrina. He had always thought that love had to be a two-way street shared between two people. When both people were set in their ways, adjusting to a partnership was difficult, even disastrous. He wasn't complaining at all, but somewhere deep within him he wanted what Trent had.

Maybe someday . . .

November 24, 2001 ~ Kandahar, Afghanistan

As a member of the 75th Ranger Regiment, Blake and his unit had been trained for every combat scenario imaginable, but nothing could have prepared him for the bitter reality of how war touched the lives of the people. After securing the landing strip south of the city, Blake and his team had been shuttled between Jalalabad, Kabul, and Kandahar, and the stench of political unrest and cultural divide was evident everywhere. He had found it a struggle to stay focused on the task when he was this close to the results of the country's history as well as airstrikes, to essentially turn off his sympathy for all the human suffering, but he relied on his brothers-in-arms and shifted back to survival mode as he geared up for the latest mission.

Under the command of Colonel Norwalk, Blake, Trent, and ten other rangers had coordinated ground logistics with the Northern Alliance, and they had been tasked with additional recon of the area before moving forward with their mission.

Blake had often wondered what aspect of war called out to him. He wasn't violent by nature, so it wasn't the sight of innocent lives wasted or the pleasure of killing. At first, it had been an outlet for his rage stemming from the attack on New York City, but with each passing day, a renewed sense of purpose coursed through his veins like burning fuel. It filled him with desire to uphold the given orders with no questions asked. Blake had found this place to be a reprieve, despite its remoteness and unfamiliarity.

At least that's what he kept telling himself. It certainly wasn't to hide from the reality that the moment this mission was over, Trent and Jennifer would be married. And it had nothing to do with him nursing his battered heart in secrecy.

Life for soldiers hung on thin thread every single day. Possible harm, and even death, plagued them, but Blake often found the thought just as comforting as it was horrifying. The military's growing distrust for the civilian population remained a disadvantage for them, but the real possibility of meeting a person on a suicide mission while they were on patrol remained the biggest threat and plenty of justification for pause. Yet they all went about their duties, pushing the potential peril out of their minds as best they could. Blake may have lived each day thinking it could be his last, but he was certain that a son serving his motherland was a damn good way to go.

Upon returning to base after a ten-hour patrol, Blake sank wearily into the lone chair remaining in the communications tent. Whispered conversations and clicking keys sounded around him as several others soldiers grabbed their tiny tastes of home in the surrounding stalls of computers and phones. He signed in and found an e-mail from Katrina.

It had been months since he'd last seen her and while they had e-mailed each other off and on, there had never been any real connection between them. Knowing how unstable his life as a soldier was, he had tried to disentangle himself from any romantic affairs before he'd shipped out.

Despite his wary outlook, he clicked on the e-mail.

> Hi Blake,
> I'm missing you. How about coming to see me once you arrive in the States?
> K

Blake sensed from Katrina's e-mail that she was reaching out, showing signs of wanting something deeper, but he tried not to give in to his loneliness and keep her at arm's length.

As impervious as he liked to believe he was, the truth was that he had been counting the days until the end of his contract for a much-needed release. Even after several weeks had passed, their communication had continued, and Katrina had promised to wait for him. The buildup was all he had to hold on to until he got home.

The more he thought about his own pleasure and release, the more he felt like a heel for taking advantage of Katrina. He had no romantic feelings for her, at least, not in a deeper sense.

Then another e-mail came, which confused him even more.

Blake,
I can't pretend anymore. I'm falling in love with you.
K

Blake leaned back in the dusty chair and stared at the computer monitor. It wasn't a surprise. He'd seen it coming.

He read and reread the damn e-mail until he was able to form some semblance of an acceptable response. Heel or no, the last thing he had ever wanted to do was hurt Katrina's feelings.

Katrina,
I won't sit here and pretend that I don't know what's going on between us, but I can't promise you anything. You can hate me for leading you on. I have nothing to give you that I haven't already done.
Blake

A response popped up not even two minutes after he had hit the send button.

That's good enough for me. I will wait for your return.
Katrina

December 12, 2001 ~ Battle of Tora Bora

Time was passing at a snail's pace in this place. What had started with the successful takeover of the landing strip two months ago had become an endless patrol that Blake counted every ticking second as a blessing. He tried to keep his fears to himself but, with each passing day, his withdrawal and silence became more noticeable.

"Yo, Connor, keep it down. I can't take all your chatterboxing, man," Trent said, smirking.

Blake folded the paper containing the mission coordinates and tucked it into his pocket. "And *you* are a shitload of fun."

"What's doing?" Trent knew him well enough to know when something was on his mind. "Remember, sharing is caring."

"I think the dust is clouding your brain. Get a medic and have the silly one-liners flushed out of your head. You're beginning to sound like a girl."

"And your long face is annoying. What happened to the jerk that I know? You look like you're knocking at hell's door." Trent's tone held a playful note, but his expression showed a fair amount of anxiousness.

Blake sobered. "I don't know. I don't have a good feeling."

"Ready, boys?" Colonel Norwalk said, halting any further banter.

The chorus of ayes rippled through the group as they piled into their assigned vehicles.

In a matter of minutes, the convoy was making its way toward the Tora Bora Mountains, which were believed to be the nesting place of the suspected mastermind of the attacks on the United States just three months prior. His exact location was the big question mark. Blake's group relied on ground intelligence while they prepared to lay siege on America's most wanted.

The wind was gusting hard and making the cold air even harsher as Trent kept them sandwiched between the two other vehicles and moving at a rapid clip to the base at the foot of the mountain.

Blake rode shotgun and surveyed the beguiling sea of green and pink opium fields with keen and watchful eyes.

In an attempt to show goodwill and avoid backlash from the farmers, the harvest had been embraced by the American troops with reluctance. The government worry had been that, with the destruction of the largest cash crop, the locals would blame the servicemen and women for their poverty.

Robert, a six-year veteran from Oklahoma, and Shane, a redneck from Kansas, were armed with sniper and assault rifles aimed just below their back windows, but more than ready to take a few teasing shots at the unusually serious Captain Connor.

"Blake, why so quiet today?" Shane asked, without missing a single chomp of his gum.

"Something's off," he muttered and kept his eyes glued forward, more alert than ever.

"You always have a bad vibe, dude. Cut it out. You give me the chills when you say shit like that." Trent pointed to another sprawling field.

Blake glanced sideways. "Then stop asking me. You guys are a bunch of sorry asses," he said, returning a wave from a child walking along the field with his mother.

The gut feeling had started long before they'd left home base, and Blake hated it. He didn't believe in a sixth sense and other superstitious crap, but this morning, for some odd reason, a prickle had kept running up and down his spine. He hadn't come across a sensation like this the whole time he'd been in the sandbox.

A loud thud reverberated in the distance.

By the sound of the explosion, Blake was pretty sure it was a rocket-propelled grenade.

The truck was slammed hard on the right-hand side, and everything seemed to pause—sounds, smells, gravity—then it registered that they were flipping end over end.

Blake was overwhelmed by the smell of fuel seconds before the gas tank burst into flames, hammering the Humvee and the men inside straight into the ground. The nature of this type of assault meant reaction had to be swift, but Blake found it difficult to act when he had to waste precious seconds finding up from down when the violent motion stopped.

"Fuck!" Blake felt like a rag doll with his limbs twisted and turned in every direction. He raised his head slowly, trying to access injuries while figuring out where the hell he was. There was no steel frame surrounding him, no window to his side, and no team members within reach. A loud roar and high pitched squeal echoed in his ears, and it felt as if his stomach might jump out his throat at even the slightest move.

He closed his hands around what should have been the dashboard only to recognize grass, rock, and dust roadway trickling between his fingers. He blinked several times and forced his breathing to slow enough to clear his head. He had been thrown from the Humvee and landed about ten feet away from the blazing crumpled lump. It must have been the adrenaline pumping in his veins that helped him stagger to his feet amid the ensuing blast that hit the other vehicles. Blood trickled from his head and he couldn't see out of one eye. He took a step forward—searing pain shot through him. He fell to the ground and saw flames on parts of his uniform. His brain barely registered what was happening, but instinct told him to roll on the ground to extinguish the heat ravaging his body. The stench of burning flesh and the confusion made him vomit.

"Help!"

It took a tremendous amount of effort for Blake to acknowledge exactly where the faint cry had originated. He summoned every ounce of his remaining energy to push his body up. He was struggling with limbs that weren't cooperating when he saw Robert crawl out of the vehicle, bloodied, with half of his left arm missing.

"Where's Trent and Shane?" Blake asked. His throat felt as though it had been sandpapered a dozen times.

"Shane's dead." Robert dragged his body away from the burning vehicle. "Stay away. The truck's going to explode," he warned before collapsing to the ground.

Blake pushed forward despite his vision flashing white and his instinct to give in to the blackness threatening him. Unable to feel much of his body, he made the excruciating forward movement to reach the burning mass. The nauseating stench of leather and other things cooking over an open flame made his stomach lurch again. He found Trent on the driver's side, bleeding. He had no time to assess the damage. He had to get his friend out.

"It's going to blow," Trent whispered, trying to push him away.

"Buddy, I'm getting you out of here." Blake grabbed Trent by his jacket, hauled him out of the fiery compartment, and dragged his friend as far away as he could.

"Jen . . ." Trent's faint voice broke into Blake's clouded haze of fear, pain, and confusion. Then Trent coughed and spat out blood.

"You're going to be okay, buddy. Hang in there." He looked down at Trent and the last thing he remembered was a blast buffeting him from behind.

The deafening screech of metal exploding, the scent of burning flesh, and Trent's plea . . .

"Take care of our girl."

And then Blake's world turned pitch black.

January 15, 2002

Four weeks after he had been airlifted to Landstuhl, Germany, in critical condition, Blake had finally been deemed stable enough to return to the States for further treatment.

His parents had flown to Europe to be with him. During the first days together, Blake had repeatedly asked them to leave so he could be alone. He couldn't bear the sight of his parents in agony at what their son had become. The nightmare was his.

As he was being prepped for the trip, he overheard the doctor talking to his parents about his condition. It was an out-of-body experience, listening to them talk about him as if he still had hope. Hope had dissipated the moment their convoy was hit with the RPG and Trent died in the blast.

"Your son is likely to experience mood swings related to PTSD," the doctor said.

He heard his mother gasp and sobbing followed. She was no stranger to the terminology, having married a soldier.

"Is he going to be okay?" Claire asked.

"The healing will be a long process. He'll need more skin grafting and physical therapy. The blindness, however, is permanent. It's going to affect his balance and his depth perception, but with therapy, he'll be able to adjust to his condition. At this point, I'm more concerned about his mental ability to recover. It is normal to have survivor's guilt, but we have to monitor his behavior. For now, I'm giving him anxiety medication. If you feel that he is exhibiting behavior that is self-destructive or he is isolating himself, you need to contact his doctor right away. The common symptoms are irritability, angry outbursts, trouble concentrating, and sleep problems. It is a natural response for a traumatized person to shut himself away from the rest of us. The effects from the trauma might be delayed, so there's a chance it won't manifest until later on. Blake will likely ignore the indicators."

Blake seethed as another sob followed the doctor's statement. It was one thing to hear the diagnosis and symptoms again and again, but having his actions dissected felt like an invasion of his privacy.

Suck it up, Connor. These are your parents. They have the right to know.

He ground his teeth, sucked in a long, deep breath, and got a grip on his emotions before asking the nurse if he could make the one phone call that had been on his mind since he had regained consciousness.

"Take care of our girl."

The last tear he'd ever shed over Trent's words made its way down his cheek. He wiped it away and cleared his throat. "Jennifer?"

"Blake? Is that you?"

"Yes . . ."

"Oh, Blake. He's gone. Trent is gone!"

It was all he could do to listen to the sound of Jennifer's pitiful crying while fighting his own demons. Trent, who had still had his entire life to live, had perished from the explosion, and he was alive.

It should have been me.

After what seemed like eternity, her sobs were reduced to hoarse whimpers, and Blake knew he had to say something. "Hey . . . you're going to be okay. Trent is now in a better place. He died doing what he loved best, and you should be proud of him."

"I-I-I . . . am . . ." She hiccupped and sniffled.

"You have to be brave and strong. I will try to call you whenever I can." It was going to be a difficult promise to fulfill.

"Thank you. Am I going to see you soon?"

Her feeble question burned worse than the explosion that had ravaged his body.

"We'll see once I get back to the States." He closed his good eye and committed the sound of her voice to memory. It was a lie and he knew it. There was no chance he'd allow Jennifer to see him this way. Not in a million years.

Another persistent tear escaped his lashes while he cursed the life he no longer wanted to live.

September 14, 2002

Every morning at six, Blake awoke to the sound of a distant neighbor's clucking chickens and barking dog. It was his usual time these days. Gone was the morning wake-up call that arrived well before sunrise from his commander, raising hell. No barked orders in a huffy military voice to get up and get ready for another day in paradise. After spending close to eight years in the military, it had been his life, his passion, and the very air that he breathed.

Contrary to what many believed, Blake hadn't joined the army because of family tradition. While his father had joined right after graduating from high school and marrying his high school sweetheart, Blake had joined the service for his own beliefs and principles. At this point, though, he couldn't even remember what those reasons had been. They didn't matter anymore. Nothing mattered anymore. The life he'd once known was over.

Regardless of what his mother said about "winning the ongoing battle with life", Blake knew he had nothing left to offer the world—not his experience, his expertise, not even his dreams.

He'd always dreamed of being in the music business, playing in small clubs, and sharing his talent and passion. He'd even pursued it in hopes that a degree in music would give him the perfect fallback plan after his stint in the military was over.

What a load of crap!

A music degree, or any degree for that matter, was useless to him now. The roadside explosion had blinded him in one eye and left him with a scarred face and an even more scarred body with one hell of a limp.

The kind of body only a mother can love and a circus can make a buck on.

The phone rang at exactly six fifteen, as it had every morning for the past nine months.

Blake rolled his eyes, dreading the pep talk waiting on the other end just like it had been every morning since he'd returned home.

She called to make sure her son had eaten, washed up, and attended therapy. Coddling wasn't something he'd ever been accustomed to, but his regrettable condition, coupled with her recent retirement, had made him an easy target for her mothering. Her daily phone call, though brief, was always geared to remind him to stop wallowing in self-pity.

Blake sighed and flicked the button on his cell. "Mom, tell me you're not going to give me a lecture again." He pulled a pillow over his face.

Wake-up calls should be outlawed, and cell phones thrown out the window. If it wasn't for emergency purposes, he'd bury the damn thing underground and forget it.

"Oh, is this a bad time?"

He jumped and dropped his cell phone in the process. "Shit." He groped for the phone until he found it next to a tattered *Playboy*. "Jennifer?"

"Yes." There was a long pause before she spoke again. "You mentioned you're always up early, so I thought I'd call."

"Yeah, I'm up." He paused, too, wondering why in the world Jennifer Owens was calling him when he'd stated that he would call her when time permitted.

"I miss him, Blake," she said.

So do I.

There was no point in saying it out loud. She knew as well as he did that Trent shouldn't have died.

"I know."

Closing his eyes, he heard Trent's voice as clear as the day he'd asked.

"Take good care of our girl."

"Why haven't you come to see me yet?"

The question startled him. Blake was supposed to have checked on her and been a guiding hand in the bleak days following his friend's death, but he hadn't kept the promise he'd made to the dying man. He gripped the cell phone tighter.

"What do you mean?" He tried to control his voice, but it still came out sounding as broken as he felt.

Jennifer sighed heavily before responding with a muffled reply. "I received a letter from him today. It was dated a few days before he died. I don't know who sent it to me, but it's his handwriting. I don't understand why he wrote at all. It's as if he knew . . ."

In his muddled thoughts, Blake tried to remember if Trent had ever mentioned anything.

The man had written several dozen letters, since e-mails and virtual chats had failed to satisfy his longing. Trent had kept paper stuffed into every pocket he could fit it and needed little more than a five-second break to start writing, including the short stops during their patrols in the streets of Kabul. He'd written about his day, what he'd seen in the field, and whatever had reminded him of her. Blake remembered cringing when the rest of the guys had taunted Trent and called him a pussy. It had been a joke to them, but Trent had a soft spot where Jennifer was concerned from the first day he'd met her.

Blake forced his right eye to focus on the ceiling, struggling for the right words. He didn't have it in him to comfort her. He was emotionally drained, aching, and just plain tired. "What did the letter say?"

"Trent apologized for not being here with me, for breaking his promise to come back home to me, alive and safe."

Although Blake wanted to offer reassurance and tell her everything was going to be all right, he wasn't able to force the words out of his mouth. There was no way in hell it ever would be all right, and he couldn't lie to her like that.

"And?" He fought against breaking down like a pathetic weakling.

If the guys could see me now.

"I shouldn't be bothering you. I—"

"Look, I'm sorry. I'm usually a good listener, but I'm just having a bad day."

Liar! It's not even seven o'clock.

"Already? But you just woke up. I know I should leave you alone, but you were closest to him. He always sounded happy whenever he talked about you."

Yeah, and it sucks, because here I am alive, and he's not. What damned good is that?

Blake scrubbed his hand over his face. "Please forgive me for being rude. It's just been rough ever since Trent—"

"I know, I just . . . I don't even know how to deal anymore. Trent told me in the letter to expect a visit from you. Why haven't you come yet?"

Damn it . . .

Jennifer had gone to bed feeling dejected and nursing a headache. When she opened her eyes to another day, the same headache lingered. The sunlight streaming through the vertical blinds hurt her eyes and made her head pound even more. She turned to face the wall, and Trent's pictures greeted her. She slipped her hand out of the covers and slid a finger across his smiling face.

She'd been young when she'd met Trent. After a devastating car accident that had claimed the lives of her parents, she had come to San Francisco to live with her spinster aunt. Trent was her next-door neighbor back then. They had become friends, and he'd helped her to cope with her loss. He was five years older than her, and by the time she had graduated from fashion design school, he'd been called for deployment.

Jennifer had suspected that Trent had feelings for her. She, on the other hand, had been uncertain of her feelings. So, when it felt as though she'd blinked only to see Trent on one knee and looking so expectant, surprise had been one of the emotions scrambling around her head.

"It would make me extremely happy if you'd be my wife." He held out an elegant solitaire ring, his sparkling green eyes imploring.

"Oh, Trent . . ."

"Please be my wife. I've loved you from the first moment I saw you.

I'm sure I can make you happy, Jen."

Tears filled her eyes. How could she say no to the man who had helped her through the toughest time of her life? She cried even though she was happy. Guilt stirred within her, because she knew her feelings for him were different. She loved him, she was sure of it, but not in the same way he loved her.

"Yes." Her answer left her stunned, and for a moment she questioned if it was driven by love or his impending departure. Then she saw his face, his smile brighter than any she'd ever seen, and she dismissed her doubts, chalking it all up to those proverbial cold feet everyone talked about.

Trent kissed her hand, and he slipped the ring on her finger.

Jennifer felt her knees buckle, and she wondered if it was from the tug at her conscience or the tickle of happiness.

"You've made me the happiest man alive." Trent kissed her tentatively at first, but then moved into a more passionate exchange that left her breathless.

When she closed her eyes, she saw Blake's face instead of Trent's. She quickly banished the vision from her head and plastered on a smile.

Once he'd arrived at his destination, they had communicated as often as possible. Trent called or came home to visit every chance he got and wrote letter after letter. By the end of his first four years, she'd collected three shoeboxes full of letters and cards from him. Each day that had passed, Jennifer had found Trent easier to love. He gave more and expected nothing in return. She had made a promise to herself—to love Trent with everything she had. They may not have had the wild heart-pounding love that stories were written about, but he was a good man and she was determined to make sure he never felt a moment's doubt in her.

During his absence, she had immersed herself in designing ready-to-wear outfits in the comfort of her aunt's apartment. When she had managed to secure a contract with a clothing store, her schedule had become hers and hers alone to set, which had been perfect when her aunt's health had taken a turn.

Aunt Debbie was her father's eldest sister. At sixty-two, she had been plagued with heart problems. Feeling as if she owed her aunt everything for spending the best years of her life taking care of an orphaned relative,

Jennifer had decided to stay and help her aunt deal with the everyday challenges she faced.

On the other side of the world and mid-tour of duty, Trent had been preparing for their wedding. They had planned to get married during his brief break between enlistment duties. His excitement had somehow rubbed off on her. Funny as it sounded, Trent had been the planner between the two of them, so she'd left all the arrangements to him and was content to follow his lead.

War and everything that came with it had proven difficult for Trent. There had been times when all he'd done during their conversations was cry. He cried for the deaths of innocent people, the poverty, the oppression, and the lost lives of his comrades.

If it hadn't been for Blake . . .

Captain Blake Connor had agreed to be his best man. Trent had talked nonstop about him during his conversations with Jennifer so it wasn't a surprise why Trent had gravitated toward him. Meeting Blake in person had left a good and lasting impression. He was sweet, laid-back, and she had seen the great friendship between Trent and him.

But fate had stepped in once again. Aunt Debbie had passed away a month before Trent's arrival. They would've gotten married as planned, but Trent, being the gentleman he was, had postponed their wedding so she could properly mourn her aunt's passing. They had decided to push everything back until he'd returned from his latest call to serve in Afghanistan.

Jennifer turned back to the window. Dealing with the pounding headache was much more bearable than looking at the pictures of Trent.

If only she could turn back the hands of time. She closed her eyes and tried to block from her mind the last letter he'd sent her.

> *"I write this letter not knowing what will happen to me. I vowed to always take care of you, but Blake will watch over you if a time ever comes when I can't. I love you, honey. Even if I can't make you happy, someone else will. Your happiness is all I want."*

Jennifer dragged her body out of bed. It was barely six in the morning, but these days, sleep often eluded her.

For days and even months following the news of Trent's death, it had been impossible for her to get a decent night's rest. Trent's smiling face often plagued her dreams as well as her waking hours. To combat her unhappiness, she had poured her heart into her work. It had been the one constant blessing left in her life, but it was coming up short lately. That's why she'd sought the comfort of the person who'd known him the best, yet the phone call with Blake yesterday had left her feeling even more bereft.

Eager to stave off another endless haze, she stepped into the shower and channeled her thoughts on the new swatches she'd bought. Jennifer tried to focus on her latest clothing designs and styles, but her mind kept wandering back to Blake and his detached behavior. Unlike Colonel Norwalk, who called often to check on her, it always felt as though the mere thought of her tortured Blake and dragging conversation out of him was a task.

Their last conversation had piqued her interest. The man was hiding something. She was sure he was still hurting from his loss, but she wondered if he would ever get around to visiting her.

If he wasn't going to make the trip, perhaps she should. Colonel Norwalk was just the man to get her there. After all, he'd promised he'd help her with anything.

Blake was the best person to help her get over Trent. He'd bring her the closure she desperately needed, and maybe she could help him a little, too.

Whether he likes it or not . . .

―∧∧―

Returning from the war had proven tough for Blake. The simple tasks he'd taken for granted in the past were now a challenge. Every turn, every move, every glance reminded him exactly how fucked up his life had become, but despite everything, he refused to surrender to his present limitations. There was also that rude awakening that the rest of the world had moved on and he had to play catch-up. Not an easy task by any means, especially with the blindness in his left eye and the multiple burns he'd sustained. According to the doctors, his limp would likely be minimal with the proper physical therapy, and it wouldn't impede his day-to-day functions.

Blake huffed and retrieved his keys for one of those day-to-day functions—his early morning drive.

As soon as he had been cleared to drive by the doctor, this daily escape had become his main source of sanity. He was right-handed, and his injuries had been limited to the left side of his body, which meant his driving leg was free to take him wherever he wanted to go.

Thank God for small favors.

His blindness was another issue. His depth perception had been compromised. Even climbing stairs was a laborious process. Driving with one eye got a bit tricky. Thanks to his father's quick thinking in attaching a fish-eye to the side of his rearview mirror, he had been able to eliminate the blind spots. The doctor had explained that for distances greater than twenty feet, people saw the world with one eye anyway. He had learned to compensate for his reduction in peripheral vision by moving his head often and following motion.

Adjusting to only one eye had taken longer to get used to. He had chosen to use an eye patch to cover his missing eye, and the damned thing was hot and uncomfortable. It also set him apart from everyone else. It was as if he wore a big neon sign, alerting everyone that he was different—a freak.

To say he'd been shocked the first time he'd looked in the mirror was an understatement. He'd recoiled at the sight and hadn't even recognized the man staring back at him, even though the doctor had declared his handiwork a success. Blake remembered gritting his teeth while he'd surveyed his newly fashioned left ear made from skin off his own butt and thigh and which was a ridiculous and incongruous accessory.

Along with the eye patch, Blake also donned a beanie to cover his head with its slow-as-a-snail growing hair and deformed ear. Year-round long-sleeve shirts and full-length pants were also a must to cover the various grafts on his body. Living in the middle of the hot desert of Lancaster, his new attire was just one more aspect that made him stick out like a sore thumb.

Calling Drew, he climbed into the Jeep with discomfort. The contracted skin on his left leg needed more work, and his repeated absences from the occupational therapy sessions were causing some stiffness.

In order to keep his field of vision clear from obstacles, Blake now made Drew sit in the backseat. His best friend scrambled into his designated spot.

Blake slowly backed his car out of the driveway, taking extra care, even though there was no traffic.

Despite his mother's protest that he should live with them during his recuperation, his father had helped him secure a rental agreement on this particular house after his discharge from Walter Reed. The location was perfect for him. Although he hadn't fulfilled his promise to Trent the way his friend had expected him to, he had been watching out for Jennifer the only way he knew how. The added bonus was that the two-bedroom bungalow was big enough for him and Drew. Since he could no longer take walks with his dog, the ample space in the backyard gave Drew enough room to run around and stretch his legs.

Trent had told him once that Jennifer had inherited her house from her aunt. An aging single story ranch-style built in the 70s, it was situated off the beaten path, a quarter of a mile away from the main artery of the city.

Blake drove the half mile to Jennifer's house and back every day without fail, even on his bad days. It had become such an obsession that he questioned whether or not it still had anything to do with his promise to a dying man.

With the midday sun beating down hard on him, he parked a few hundred yards away and sat there, thinking and watching.

Drew moved about the small confines of the cab, aching to jump out.

"Sit, Drew," he said.

Despite the dog's eagerness to bolt, he followed Blake's order and sat still. His panting was the lone sound in the vehicle.

Blake pulled his beanie down a fraction and his heart slammed hard against his chest when he saw a figure emerge from the garage. Although his eye was still adjusting to the distance, he was sure it was Jennifer. Gripping the steering wheel, he watched as she walked down to the curb and threw something in the garbage can. He slid lower in his seat when she shielded her eyes from the sun and turned right in the direction of his parked Jeep.

After a few moments, she walked back in the house, and Blake sighed in relief. The last thing he needed was to blow his cover. His stalker act would definitely send her running to the cops.

He started the car, stepped on the gas, and hoped Jennifer wasn't peeking out her window.

—◦◦◦—

"Colonel Norwalk? Jennifer Owens here."

"Jennifer! How are you, my child?"

She smiled. Colonel Lance Norwalk called everyone "child." She remembered that from Trent's stories. "I'm fine, and yourself?"

"I'm doing great, although my hips are killing me. My doctor said I'll live," he said, chuckling.

"Are you shipping out anytime soon?" It was a staple of any conversation with an active duty soldier.

Jennifer stared out the window and noticed the Jeep she'd seen earlier streak by. She tried to see who was driving, but some sort of hat concealed the driver's face. It had been a little unnerving to see an unfamiliar vehicle on her road, so she took note of the brown vehicle with the word *Wrangler* emblazoned on the left side, just in case.

"The missus is urging me to retire. I still have a few years left in this old body of mine, so I think I'll serve my remaining years." The older man's tenor had a calming effect on her, just like Blake's deep, bass voice. "What can I do for you, child? I'm sure you didn't call just to ask an old man how he's doing."

"I wanted to ask you about Captain Blake Connor." She heard a sharp sigh at the other end of the line.

"You know we are not at liberty to disclose anything about a fellow soldier."

Jennifer had expected the answer, so she had already come up with an argument. "Trent left a few things, and I wanted to send them to Blake. I lost his phone number, and I don't know how else to get in touch with him."

Liar.

Feeling a bit nervous, she chewed on her bottom lip while waiting for Colonel Norwalk's response. He knew how close the guys had all been, so there was always a chance.

"You know how Blake cherishes his privacy after what happe—"

"What happened to him?" Her heart thrummed against her ribs as she tried to wait out the silence on the other end of the line. Her conversation with Blake the day before came into focus. He'd mentioned having a bad day.

"I'm sorry, but it's none of my business. As I said, I'm not at liberty to divulge Army matters to anyone, but I'll give you his address. Hold on, let me get it for you."

Jennifer sighed and rummaged in her drawer for a pen and paper.

A click sounded just before the colonel came back on the line. "Here . . . looks like he moved when he returned to the States. You ready?"

As Captain Norwalk recited the address, Jennifer's hand began to tremble. She wrote down everything, feeling as if someone had doused her with cold water.

"Thank you." Her voice sounded brittle even to her own ears.

"You're welcome. Call me anytime you need anything, child."

"I will." She closed her eyes, trying to make sense of the newfound information.

He's here.

Questions began running through her mind. The sooner she got some answers the better off she would be, with or without Blake's friendship.

"If you ever get in touch with my boy, tell him I want him back. Desk job isn't so bad. Tell him to reconsider." The man's tone was laden with remorse.

"I'll make sure your message is delivered as soon as possible."

And in person.

They hung up soon after, and she sat at her desk, pondering her next move.

Blake drove straight to the rehab center from Jennifer's house. With a huff of disgust at his carelessness, he pounded the steering wheel.

She could've seen him that close to her house. Next time, he needed to be more careful.

He attached the leash to Drew's collar and walked to the front entrance of the building where Drew was supposed to wait for him to complete another session of painful exercises to loosen up his constricted muscles.

Given that he'd been plagued with anxiety attacks, the doctor had proclaimed him a good candidate for a companion dog. Voilà, Drew was promoted to elite status and could now enter any establishment with him. If he'd had a choice, Blake would have skipped the therapy session altogether, but the noticeable change in his range of motion might well mean he had put off therapy too long this time.

Sam Sweeney met him at the door, undoubtedly evaluating his mood as they made their way to a private therapy room.

Blake looked around, taking inventory of the few people in the room. Early morning sessions were far better than late ones, since he didn't particularly cherish the curious stares or the pitying glances that came his way. Although Sam hadn't asked too many questions, Blake was sure the therapist understood his reluctance to attend the sessions. Sam had served in the military, too, and as an ex-marine, there was no question he'd been exposed to enough injuries to give him a lifetime of sleepless nights and recurring nightmares. He would know how Blake felt.

"Good morning, man. Glad you showed up today." Sam gestured to the chair opposite his desk. "Hello there, Drew." He patted the furry head as Drew passed.

"Thanks." Blake sat down with a grunt.

Just as he had been trained to do, Drew settled in close to him.

Sam didn't waste time. "So . . . tell me how you feel today."

Why is small talk so awkward?

Blake adjusted his legs in front of him.

Sam chortled.

"Um, let's see . . . I'm stiff and can't move in this damn body. I ache everywhere, and I'm bored to death. And how are you today?" Blake smirked and cocked an eyebrow.

"I'm good. Could be better, could be worse."

Same damn answer every time he saw the guy.

Blake couldn't help but grin, finding it difficult to dislike Sam. As much as he'd tried to keep his distance from the large man in his late forties with a likeable personality, quick wit, and admirable patience, the two men had hit it off from day one. They spoke the same language and had seen the worst in their stints in the military. Blake liked the guy, but not enough to show up like he should. He abhorred the monster he'd turned into, and being reminded of it every day was too much to bear.

"Good. Now, can we skip the bullshit and get this session started?"

Sam chuckled but narrowed his green eyes as he caught Blake flinching. "We'll start with your hand and arm this morning."

Blake knew the drill by heart. He offered his healing hand, and Sam took a tube of moisturizer to the affected areas. Blake closed his eyes as Sam began massaging. The soothing sensation of the cream seeped through his cracked skin and provided a cool relief to the dryness.

Conscientious massage could be effective in limited areas of scarring. The convenience of having a family member performing the massage would eliminate unnecessary visits. In Blake's situation, he had to do the massaging himself. Between limited mobility and refusal to stay consistent, he hadn't had much luck in that particular area. He had refused to get his parents involved, and Katrina was barely more than a distant memory these days. Ideally, the technique should have been performed several times each day.

"Are you wearing your compression vest?" Sam was quick to catch every reaction.

"I forgot," Blake said, not even bothering to meet the other man's gaze.

Sam snorted. "Sure . . . I told you already, compression garments must be worn twenty-four-seven until scarring decreases. It takes twelve to eighteen months after an injury before you can shed them. You're not taking your well-being seriously." Sam shook his head, appearing disappointed with Blake's obvious lack of cooperation.

Blake had heard all the cautions, and as much as he wanted to disregard Sam's claim, he realized the man was right. The trouble was his inability to look at his body in the mirror. There were too many changes and damage he couldn't bear to see.

"I'll start wearing the damn vest when I get home."

"Tell me, what do you do in your spare time?" Sam acted as if he was oblivious to Blake's need for silence.

Blake ground his teeth and tried to choose his words carefully. "Do I have to remind you that I don't work anymore? Spare time is all I've got. I watch sitcoms, soaps, and a lot of those stupid infomercials, if that's what you want to know." He gave Sam a clear *fuck off* warning glare, but the older guy seemed intent on getting under his skin today.

"Well . . . that doesn't sound like fun. Why don't you meet me at The Cage after work today? The place is cool, dark, and no-nonsense. No one pays attention to anyone. Besides, they have a free mic night. Anyone can come on stage and perform. Nothing doing, just hang out with me."

Blake's biggest mistake had been mentioning once to Sam his disgust at being stared at and his passion for music. These days, the other man seemed hell-bent on making sure he performed his Mother Teresa duties by getting Blake out of the house and back into circulation.

"No, thanks." Blake shook his head.

"You know better. I won't take no for an answer. I'll let it go today, but I'm not going to stop asking. Don't forget I know where you live, and I got your cell number, too." Sam grinned and his eyes glittered.

"You can try annoying me, but it won't work." Blake seethed when he recognized the determination in Sam's face, and he knew better than to argue. The man had been in the military for a long time. Persistence and patience came with the territory.

"Just saying." Sam finished the hand massage and worked on the rest of Blake's left arm.

Blake kept his eyes closed and his mouth shut while Sam worked on the rest of his limbs. It was the part of therapy that he detested the most. Looking at his body in the mirror was one thing, letting another person see his scars and what was left of his body was too much for him.

Sam remained quiet, whistling and humming while he worked.

After their session, Blake felt a remarkable difference in his range of motion, although he refused to admit to it. Stubborn was his middle name, after all, and anger had taken up permanent residence in his psyche.

Drew jumped up the minute Blake set out to leave.

The dog had been a puppy when Blake had begun serving in the military. Now at seven years old, Drew still had spring in his step despite the noticeable swelling on his front legs—the onset of arthritis, according to his veterinarian.

Wagging his tail, Drew licked Blake's hand as soon as he took the leash.

"Hey, boy, ready to go?" Blake murmured, giving his pal a thorough rubdown on his back and neck.

The minute they walked out of the air-conditioned building, searing heat hit Blake full blast. Only ten in the morning, and the temperature tipped the nineties. They hustled to the Jeep where Blake began pulling the soft top back. The leather seat was way too hot to sit on. He fanned the material to help cool it down, giving it several more minutes before he could manage to bear sitting on the hot surface.

He drove to town and grabbed some food before heading home. His body began reacting to the blistering heat, making him a little lightheaded. It was a sure sign that he needed cooler temperatures right away.

What a joke.

The last place one would expect to find a burn victim was living in a sweltering town that boasted cacti, tumbleweeds, and mile after mile of barren land.

Once he reached home, he snagged his take-out burrito and a glass of iced tea, and settled into the lounger perfectly situated in the cool shade of his backyard, while Drew sprawled out in contentment by his feet. Blake shed his beanie but not his eye patch. Months hadn't helped him get used to the empty eye socket, and he doubted he ever would be. In a few weeks, he would be meeting with an ocularist to get fitted with an artificial eye. He'd still be blind, but at least he wouldn't have to garner stares because he looked like a misplaced pirate. Pretending to be normal was taxing, but if he ever had a sliver of desire to rejoin the rest of the world, he should at least *try* to fit in.

Not that I care.

With a sigh, he downed the remaining iced tea.

The doorbell rang.

Persistent bastard!

Blake padded past the living room and yanked the front open. "Can't you take no for an answer? Shove your shit down your throat and scram!" Blake almost stumbled backward when he realized it wasn't Sam's face on the other side, but Jennifer's.

God, she looks better every time.

Her smile faded and she gasped.

He couldn't help wondering if it was due to his not-so-warm welcome or his appearance.

Two guesses, and the first don't count.

"What are you doing here?" The moment the words left his mouth, he wished he could take them back and crawl under the nearest rock.

"Blake?"

His shock finally dissipated and anger began to seep in. "I asked you what you're doing here." He'd never wanted her to feel pity for him.

"I—"

"Go home. There's nothing for us to say to each other." Blake had started to push the door closed when he saw her expression turn from wretched to livid in a matter of seconds.

Jennifer moved forward and wedged her foot against the door to stop him from closing it on her. "Trent was wrong about you. He kept telling me what a nice person you were, how helpful. Not only have you ignored me, ignored losing Trent, but you're also rude."

"I don't care what I am. You're not welcome here. Go home, Jennifer."

His words must've struck a chord because Jennifer took a step back without saying another word and turned away, but not before he saw tears trickle down her cheeks.

I'm sor—no! No turning back. It has to be this way.

Blake slammed the door behind him and stormed back to the patio when he heard her car drive off. He plopped onto the patio chair with unrestrained anger.

How in the hell did she find me? She's better off thinking I'm a prick.

With a grunt of self-reproach, he buried his face in his hands. "I'm so sorry, Trent. I can't do it, buddy."

Blake lay on his bed tossing, turning, and staring into the darkness while replaying Jennifer's unannounced visit. He cursed his inexcusable rudeness and felt remorse upon remembering her hurt expression. His actions were unforgivable, and he wouldn't blame her if she never spoke to him again.

Groaning, he reached for the bottle of sleeping pills on his nightstand. Tonight he needed the help. He crushed the pill with his teeth, turned on the lamp, picked up the *Playboy* from the floor, and started ruffling through the pages.

" 'What must a man do these days to get laid?' Okay, not the article I should be reading right now." He groaned and flipped past several bunnies gracing the pages in their cuddly pompom tails and adorable headpieces, and he was reminded of his vow of celibacy. He'd be a hypocrite to say missing that aspect in his life didn't bother him, but with his injuries, his bum eye, and patches of shit over his entire left side . . .

Not even if I paid 'em.

His heart lurched and his stomach tightened at the memory of Katrina.

———

Jennifer awoke with a start. She heard the tail end of her scream and struggled to sit up. Somehow, nightmares had spared her, even in the months immediately following Trent's death.

Why now? And why Blake?

She scrambled out of bed and hurried to the bathroom to wash her face and clear the remnants of the godforsaken dream.

Wiping her face dry, she glanced at her reflection. Mottled cheeks, puffy eyes, and an unhappy expression stared back at her. "You're crazy, Jen."

Swallowing the lump in her throat, she tried to push the haunting thoughts away. She'd dreamt of Blake coming home from the war, his uniform tattered, his face burned beyond recognition, yet she'd welcomed him with open arms. Instead of stepping into her embrace, he had turned away and walked back to a burning car. He had pulled out a body from the fiery wreckage and brought a dead soldier back to her.

"No . . ."

"I'm so sorry. I tried. I was hoping it was me instead of him." Tears *trickled from his eyes but fizzled as soon as they touched his burning cheeks.*

"Blake . . . no, not you."

"It was either Trent or me. He gave up. His heart gave out." His broken *sobs had ripped through her in the dream.* *"I'm sorry, Jennifer."*

She closed her eyes and covered her ears, trying to block out the images and the remains of her dream from her mind. A cry rose in her throat and a new breed of pain gripped her. The helpless kind of ache she hadn't felt before. Her heart rammed against her ribcage at the painful reminder of two lives ensconced by the bitter effects of the war.

Staggering back to her room, she knelt down by the bed and pulled a box containing pictures from underneath. Pictures she had avoided looking at for fear of hurting all over again. It seemed as if the dream and seeing Blake again had opened a well of sorrow she'd fought hard to forget.

She opened the box to see a photo taken in 2009, according to Trent's scribble on the back of the picture. The image of two grinning men with an arm on the other's shoulder, each holding a bottle of beer, greeted her.

Trent had been good-looking in a *GQ* kind of way, while Blake had a more rugged appeal with piercing blue eyes that stared right through her. He and Trent had been almost the exact same height, same build—muscular, arresting, and both incredibly pleasing to the eye. While Trent's open smile reached ear to ear, Blake's hinted at some secret.

Jennifer sank to the floor, still staring at the picture.

The man she had seen yesterday was different. Not because of the noticeable scars on his neck and chin or the eye patch he wore, but because of the hostility emanating from him. His dismissal of her and his rudeness was all part of the wall he'd built around himself to hide his confusion and pain.

She didn't know Blake well, but when she thought of all he'd done for Trent in the past her anger eased and she felt compelled to return the favor.

What can I do when he's made it clear he wants nothing to do with me?

Through it all, one question kept nagging—how had he ended up in the same city? Of course, that one caused a chain reaction of questions to sprout up. How long had they been neighbors? She was sure the Jeep she had spotted parked in front of his house was the same one she'd seen racing past her house yesterday. Had Blake been watching her all along? She had questions piling on top of each other and the only person who had the answers wanted nothing to do with her.

There was a faint knocking at her door.

She threw the picture on her bed and pushed the box back in its hiding place. Pulling her robe tightly around her, she ran toward the door as she wiped the errant tears away.

Leaving a little gap but not releasing the chain bolt, she peered out and gasped.

Blake, hands buried in his pockets and one-eyed piercing gaze, regarded her with intensity. "I believe I owe you an apology."

Jennifer remained glued behind the door, watching Blake through the small crack that separated them. She must've have stared long enough to make Blake uncomfortable because he shifted and looked at her expectantly.

She only blinked twice in reply, and he sighed and turned back toward the door.

Say something!

"You're not the same man I met a year ago. You're an angry man and very, very rude." Not what she'd intended to say, but the words were out of her mouth before she'd had the chance to think.

Blake whipped his body around, his eye flickering. "I'm not at all what Trent painted me out to be." His voice was gravelly, and there was a hint of sadness Jennifer recognized right away.

"Trent was never wrong, but I suppose there's always a first time." Another one of those things she wouldn't have said under normal circumstances, but this wasn't even remotely normal. She pushed the chain lock to open, stepped past the threshold, and out the door.

He narrowed his uncovered eye into a slit and watched her just long enough to make her squirm. "I apologized already. I could've handled your uninvited visit better."

She gaped and her blood began to boil.

The nerve of this . . . this . . .

She stepped forward to give him a piece of her mind but stopped short when she realized this was about to turn into fighting like little children in front of her house.

"I should have called before I came, but since we are *neighbors* . . . I thought it was neighborly to pop in and say, 'hi.' "

Blake's jaw clenched, and she thought she heard him huff. His insolent gaze traveled from her face to her ratty robe, lingering around the area of her breasts, before slipping to her bare feet.

How dare he! As if I'm something to eat.

She felt a frisson of anger flush within and tilted her chin up.

His mouth twitched upward.

If he felt uneasy with her reference to their living proximity, he showed no signs, and it only made her angrier.

"This is a free country. I chose to live in a town where my neighbor doesn't have to know my name." He turned around and moved across the gravel drive toward a Jeep with a dog in the seat waiting for him.

"Where are you going?" She took several steps down her small porch, but the searing heat of the pavement under her bare feet made her jump back.

Blake glanced over his shoulder, his lips quirking into a sneer. "I came to apologize and I did. I'm going home." He swung his right leg into the driver's seat with obvious effort. Half seated, he pulled his left leg up. He shot her a glare, as if daring her to say something.

You pompous ass!

Jennifer felt the curse working its way out of her mouth and, before she could stop herself, the words spilled out. "If you made the trip, the least I can do is offer you a cup of coffee."

What the—okay, not where I saw that going.

Blake stared out the windshield with a hard scowl. It took another moment before his shoulders relaxed.

"You can bring your dog, too." She stepped inside and gripped the doorknob, hoping he'd say yes.

What's gotten into me?

Sure, he had been Trent's friend, but this man had made it clear he wanted nothing to do with her. He'd come to apologize, and he'd done just that.

To her surprise, he heaved his body out of his Jeep, wincing at the same time.

She could only imagine his physical pain. She had so many questions, but common sense told her she'd better hold them for another time.

"Drew, come, boy." The bass of his voice lacked the hostile tone he had used on her. It sounded almost mellow, like a caress.

The large dog jumped from the backseat onto the hot pavement and looked up at his master.

With a noticeable limp, Blake walked back to her porch, dog on his heels, and took the few steps one at a time.

She had no medical background, but it was easy to see his caution had something to do with his visual impairment.

She stayed still, trying not to stare, and restrained herself from offering help. Once he made it up the steps, she stepped back and let him walk in. When his arm accidentally brushed against hers, she shivered despite the hot day. He smelled like mint and honest-to-goodness male sweat.

Get a grip, Jennifer.

He stood in the middle of the room with the powerful looking animal next to him and waited for her.

She stepped to his right, his good side, and stopped short when it registered what she'd done. She had no idea why.

Why do I care when he seems hell-bent on making me uncomfortable?

Jennifer cleared her throat and gestured toward the chair. "Have a seat. Let me start the coffee."

Blake didn't respond nor did he move.

Instead of running to the kitchen to start the pot, she headed toward her bedroom. She heard a grunt followed by the squishing sound of the sofa cushions as soon as she was out of view.

Running to her walk-in closet, she pulled out a pair of denim shorts and a white cotton T-shirt. After changing, she stepped into the bathroom to comb her bed-head hair and tied it into a high ponytail. Taking a deep breath and settling her fluctuating emotions, she passed by the living room on her way to the kitchen.

The Doberman sat on the floor next to Blake who sat on the sofa, ramrod straight, with his gaze fixed on picture frames on the mantel, and he didn't seem to notice her passing by.

She disappeared into the kitchen and grabbed the carafe. She busied herself with preparing the coffee while caught in a daze. She glanced at the clock and debated whether to return to the living room and sit with Blake while the coffee percolated. Deciding against it, she retrieved the powdered creamer and sugar containers from the cupboard and placed them with the exquisite antique cups and matching saucers left to her by Aunt Debbie.

—⁓—

Thank God, Jennifer's house was cool. Between his cotton, long-sleeved shirt, his beanie, and the jeans, he looked like one of those wandering transients. He came complete with a dog, too. Blake surveyed the entire room, taking in every detail.

Her place seemed homey. There were books everywhere, on the table, by the sofa where he sat, and piled in a neat row next to picture frames by the end table. Several mannequins were propped against the wall with rolls of fabrics next to them. The eclectic fireplace was surrounded by green stones synonymous with the 70s era.

Looking at the hearth with the blackened edges, he imagined Jennifer sitting by the fire during cold winter nights, alone. His heart constricted at the unhappy picture.

The mantel held several framed photographs and he strained to see them. Squinting, one particular photo caught his attention.

Trent was grinning happily, but not at the camera. He was gazing down at Jennifer, who wore a small smile and stared right into the camera's lens, her expressive eyes misty. Trent held her hand while his other hand encircled her waist.

Blake blinked and shifted his attention to the rest of the room, immersing in the warmth of being under the same roof with her. Trent had told him everything there was to know about this beautiful and caring woman. In a strange way, Blake felt as though he'd known her for years. Truth was, he barely knew her and outside of their shared time with Trent, he'd been a total ass to her . . . nothing to be proud of.

The scent of hazelnut wafted into the living room, followed by a beeping sound.

He brought his mind back where it should be and leaned against the sofa, trying his best to look relaxed. His breath caught in his throat as her full form stopped a few feet away—the exact range to catch every single one of her features in perfect focus.

Although she seemed to have lost weight, she still had one of those knockout bodies that made other females jealous. Her fraying denim shorts complemented her long legs that tapered at the ankles, making her even sexier and soft looking.

Blake groaned.

How long has it been since . . .

"Coffee's ready. Why don't we have it in the other room where the chairs are much more comfortable?" She turned around, clearly expecting him to follow.

His eyes landed on her full and tight backside filling her shorts in all the right places.

Fuck it, Connor.

He pushed his body off the sofa. The short inactivity had already settled his skin into a tight constriction, making the process of getting up more difficult. He cursed at the pain of stretching his legs.

Jennifer halted and threw him a worried glance.

"Go . . ." He gestured with a hand. It was rude, but he didn't even know how to start explaining his caveman attitude to her. He followed her to the other room, grumbling at the discomfort.

Drew didn't move from his spot when he caught Blake's quick wave to stay.

The kitchen was another throwback to the 70s. The dark wood cabinets and the fluorescent lighting overhead reminded him of his parents' home.

"Have a seat. How would you like your coffee?" Jennifer proceeded to the counter and started pouring.

"One teaspoon of sugar, please. No cream." He settled into a bright yellow leatherette chair. His buttocks appreciated the firm but comfortable cushion, and he had to grudgingly acknowledge Jennifer's attention to details.

She came back with two fragile-looking cups set in tiny saucers and placed them on the table. She sat opposite him in the small dinette, not bothering to look at him.

"Thanks," he said, reaching for the little cup.

"You're welcome." Her voice was low and had a sweet ring to it.

He eyed the tiny handle and wondered how in the hell he was going to get his finger through the small opening. Like an uncivilized grunt, he grabbed the bowl of the cup and stiffened. The scalding heat of the porcelain left him motionless.

As though he had no control over his limbs, his hand twitched and the cup fell to the table with a loud clang. "I'm sorry." He brought the hand to his mouth and blew on it. He hated looking like a pansy in front of a woman, or anyone for that matter, and his anger boiled over at the idea that she had seen him flinch.

Without a word, Jennifer reached across the small table and pulled on his arm.

He tensed at her searing touch.

She applied pressure on his arm until he relented. With care, she turned his palm and started massaging it.

The sensation was electric. She rendered him weak and vulnerable.

For Pete's sake! When did I become such a pussy?

"You don't have—"

"Oh, be quiet. You almost burned yourself."

Her statement struck a sensitive chord. He cocked an eyebrow. "If you used a cup that could fit a normal finger, this wouldn't have happened." He yanked his hand from her grasp and stood up. He ignored the pain radiating throughout his legs. "Thanks for the coffee and enjoy the rest of your day."

Without a backward glance, he stormed out of the room, whistled once on his way toward the front door, and headed for his Jeep.

Drew followed behind him.

He had no business drinking coffee in her kitchen, and without a doubt, he had no right to enjoy the warmth of her touch.

Damn his life to high heaven.

At the crack of dawn, Jennifer was up and ready to go. She had a nine o'clock presentation in LA that her agent had scheduled with a new client. This was one of the rare situations when she left the house.

The trip doubled as a perfect excuse to meet up with Coleen. Ever since she'd moved to Lancaster, and Coleen had relocated to San Diego after she'd gotten married, finding opportunities to see each other had been close to impossible. Although they often spoke on the phone, nothing could beat a face-to-face gossip session. Los Angeles was the perfect meeting spot, being the halfway point between their residences.

Still smarting from Blake's abrupt departure the day before, Jennifer hadn't gotten enough sleep. She had tossed and turned, rewinding every detail in her head, remembering his reactions and his misplaced anger. If she hadn't met him before and seen the sweet smile not only tilting his lips but also lighting his eyes, she would have discounted him as a rude prick.

There had to be a reason behind his rage, and while she'd love to find it, there was little chance she'd be knocking on his door again. Not only had he made it clear that she repulsed him, but his actions left no doubt that he preferred to be alone.

"So be it!" she said out loud, punctuating her determination with one good nod.

The hour-and-a-half drive to West LA was uneventful, with light traffic and parking readily available. It was going to be a good day.

Feeling confident, she strode into the high-rise building, took the elevator to the nineteenth floor, and was promptly whisked to the conference room.

Her agent, Matt Crest, was already seated in one of the plush leather chairs. He stood up and smiled easily as she breezed in. "Jenny . . . you're still pretty and punctual. What a combination." He walked forward and gave her a peck on the cheek.

She smelled his aftershave and wrinkled her nose. "And you're still trying to flatter my socks off, Matthew." She took the chair next to him and placed her briefcase on top of the mahogany table. "How many clients do we have to convince today?"

"Just one buyer from Maxie's. If Ms. Holloway likes your designs and orders all of them, then we are set for the rest of the year." Matthew grinned and leaned back on the chair.

"I prepared ten sketches, and I took pictures of each style draped on mannequins. I also brought some samples of the fabrics for her inspection." She gave Matt a nervous smile.

"I'm positive we'll hit our target today."

Within a few minutes, a woman in her thirties walked in, dressed in an impeccable two-piece beige suit. She introduced herself and small talk preceded the presentation.

Once Jennifer got into the staging aspect, she took off explaining the designs for the next hour. Passing her sketches from Ms. Holloway to Matt, she kept a steady pace on her sales pitch concerning the materials, the intricate details of each style, and the intended market for her creations.

Ms. Holloway seemed impressed, but instead of giving her opinion on the designs, the fashion buyer promised she'd call by the end of the week with her decision.

Matthew requested Jennifer wait for him in the lobby. He emerged from the conference room looking smug.

"So . . ." She followed him to the elevator. "What do you think?"

Matthew put an arm around her shoulder and pulled her close, and a feeling of elation washed through her. "I don't want to get your hopes up, but I think we caught a fish *this* big." He gestured with his free hand, and they laughed together.

Though Matt was technically her agent, they had gone to fashion school together. He had opted to pursue the business side of the trade while she had gone after her lifelong dream of designing ready-to-wear clothing. She intended to stretch her wings by getting into *haute couture* in the future, but for now, she was content with designing for a major clothing chain. So far, their venture together had been successful. Jennifer worked at her own schedule and pace while he scoured for clients.

Back in the day, few straight men forayed into the fashion world, and many a girl had debated exactly which side of the argument Matt landed on. There had been a few occasions when Jennifer had felt sexual tension emanating from him, but he'd never acted on it. She had brushed the feelings away as her overactive imagination running wild. Even with his attractive features, she'd felt no draw toward him. She had always been fond of Matthew and never once felt threatened by his company. Jennifer considered him one of the few people she trusted.

He promised to call her as soon as he heard from the prospective client.

After a few minutes of banter in the parking lot, they drove their separate ways.

Just past noon, Jennifer found Coleen sitting at a corner booth of the bustling restaurant where they'd agreed to meet.

With a wave, Coleen jumped from her seat and gave her a warm hug. "Jenny! It's been a long time, girlfriend! I've missed you so much." Coleen squealed in her high-pitched voice, garnering stares from other diners.

"I missed you, too. How long has it been?"

They settled in the booth opposite each other and held hands, both grinning with enthusiasm.

"Um . . . I think it's been too long." Coleen smiled and her blue eyes twinkled.

"I know that look. What are you keeping from me?" Jennifer tugged her friend's hand. It wouldn't be difficult to get her best friend to sing like a canary.

Coleen burst into fits of giggles. "I'm pregnant!" Her eyes misted and her mouth stretched from ear to ear.

Jennifer's jaw dropped a full three seconds before she blinked, tugged Coleen's hand, dragging her out of her seat, and they both started jumping up and down while hugging each other.

"Oh my God! Oh my God! Congratulations! When are you due?"

"Around Christmas. Can you believe it?" Pure joy radiated from Coleen's face.

Jennifer couldn't help but feel a pang of jealousy. Not for Coleen's good fortune, but for her own situation. She had been so close to having it all, only to have it all feel so far away. "Of course I can. You're going to have a Christmas baby. It's perfect."

They broke into a fit of giggles, leaning into each other as they wiped their tears, when they noticed everyone staring at them.

Coleen gasped for breath and cleared her throat, sitting down again and regaining her composure. "Jen . . . I want to ask you something."

"Anything."

"Will you be the baby's godmother?" The hopeful look on Coleen's face made Jennifer ache.

Coleen and her husband, Mike, were Catholics. They believed in the whole godparents-acting-as-second-parents deal, especially during the child's formative years. Jennifer, on the other hand, was a "Christmas Catholic" as Aunt Debbie used to joke, since her attendance was limited to holidays and special occasions.

Even if she never had a child of her own, she would still have someone to nurture. "Of course. I'd be honored."

After their orders were placed, Coleen began her litany of questions. As her closest friend, Coleen felt the need to ensure Jennifer's well-being and happiness. Jennifer knew it and had accepted her friend's mothering with resignation.

Their food came, and within minutes they were stuffing themselves and launching into another round of catching up. Jennifer hadn't intended to divulge her trip to Blake's house and his subsequent visit, but once she'd started talking about Trent, she hadn't been able to stop the snowball effect.

"Are you telling me that Blake lives not even a mile away from you?" Coleen shuddered. "He sounds like a stalker to me."

Jennifer nodded then shook her head. "Yes, we're neighbors, but I don't think he is a stalker. I mean—look . . . he doesn't want to have anything to do with me. He got upset when I showed up at his doorstep."

Coleen wasn't convinced. "Sure, he's trying to show you that he isn't interested, but why, in heaven's name, would he pick a house close to yours? Have you ever thought about it?"

"Of course I thought about it. I told you about Trent's letter, didn't I?"

Coleen nodded.

"Well, Trent said Blake would be watching out for me, and that's what he's doing." It made perfect sense to Jennifer. Besides, she wasn't prepared to think of Blake as a stalker. She couldn't imagine why a man like him would stalk his best friend's fiancée.

Ex-fiancée.

"Whatever." Coleen still looked doubtful. "I want you to call me if you suspect anything out of the ordinary."

Jennifer giggled. "And what will you do? Drive four hours at breakneck speed to clobber him?"

Coleen snorted. "I can do that, too, but I'm thinking more in terms of calling the cops and reporting a good-looking stalker."

Jennifer put her fork down. "You're one crazy woman." She shook her head and then sobered. "You know, I think he's bitter because of what he is going through now."

"What are you talking about?" Colleen rested her elbows on the table and leaned forward.

"I don't have all the details but judging from his physical injuries, I think it's bothering him. Trent had never mentioned that Blake had a temper. The little bit of time I actually spent around him, he seemed like a cool guy. Always smiling, cutting up, and teasing Trent. I think it's related to the pain he's experiencing."

"Hmm . . ." Colleen seemed lost in thought as she moved the food around her plate with her fork. "Don't tell me that you're planning to hold his hands while he goes through his rough patch. Remember, you're not a doctor. You have no idea what he's been through. Don't pretend to understand when you don't. These guys returning from the wars have scars deeper than any wounds we see. For all you know, Blake's suffering from some psychological problem."

"Don't worry about me. I think Blake is harmless." Somehow, she was sure of it, but Jennifer tucked Coleen's words away for more thought later.

"Just a word of caution, girlfriend. He seemed like he's carrying a lot of baggage, and you're still grieving. It sounds like the making of a tragic love story." Colleen held her gaze, as if sizing up her mental well-being.

"Oh, c'mon. Don't play mother hen with me." Jennifer wagged a finger at her best friend.

"I trust you to make a good call. Don't fall for this guy because you pity him or you're aching for Trent." Coleen put her fork down, reached across the table, and gave Jennifer's hand a light squeeze.

"Thanks for your concern. I don't intend to get involved with anyone right now. Certainly not a man with issues and probable post-traumatic stress disorder." Jennifer sounded so sure, and she wondered if she was trying to convince Coleen or herself.

They chatted for another two hours, while attacking a slice of black forest cake and lingering over coffee. After settling their check, they walked around the promenade to window shop. It was a little past seven in the evening by the time they hugged and said their goodbyes. Jennifer was in high spirits when she eased her car onto the freeway for the long drive home.

Jennifer slipped her shoes off the moment she crossed her threshold, tired from the whole day of wearing high heels. She'd gotten so used to working at home in her pajamas and flip-flops.

She proceeded down the darkened hallway into her bedroom and heard a crunch seconds before an odd searing pain shot through her right foot.

"Ow." She hobbled toward the light switch.

Once the room was bathed in light, she gasped. Her bedroom was in utter disarray. Looking down at her foot, she saw blood pooling on the floor underneath it. Pain radiated up her leg, and she wobbled to sit on the bed. She tried assessing the extent of her injury, but with the steady stream of blood, it was difficult to see the size of the gash on her foot.

A wave of panic gripped her while she glanced around the room. She could see that her walk-in closet had been turned upside down. Drawers had been opened and clothes were strewn everywhere. The glass she'd stepped on had been an antique vase once belonging to her aunt.

Reaching for the phone on her nightstand, she dialed 911. Once she knew help had been dispatched, belated tears of shock overcame her. She was in a full fit of hysteria by the time the first cop showed up.

When the responding officer saw the blood on the floor, he radioed for medical assistance and helped her into the living room. He wrapped her foot with a towel he had snagged from the bathroom and propped her leg on the coffee table.

The medics arrived a few minutes later and started assessing her injury.

Another squad car pulled up her driveway, and two officers walked into the living room. Each one identified himself and went about checking the rest of the house and inspecting the broken window.

Officer Cortez, the first officer on the scene, sat on the sofa opposite her after he conferred with the medic. "You need to go to the emergency room to get that foot stitched up. You also need to take inventory of your things. See what's missing. Check with your credit card company for any unauthorized charges. I suggest you cancel the credit cards and request new ones, just in case the burglar got a hold of your account information. We'll be dusting for fingerprints soon to see if we can get a match in our system."

Before she could answer, loud voices sounded from the garage.

Officer Cortez stood up to check, but Blake stormed in the room, followed closely by another officer.

—◦—

Regardless of what had happened yesterday, Blake knew he wouldn't rest easy until he made one more drive by Jennifer's house. He had no intention of knocking on her door. Some things, and people, were better left alone, and Jennifer deserved better . . . much better.

When he neared her house, however, he saw flashing lights synonymous with emergency vehicles. He felt his stomach clench and his gut twist, while terrible scenarios played in his head. He stomped on the gas and, with squealing tires, announced his arrival from a block away. He parked as close as he could get and jumped out.

An officer came forward, blocking his way as he headed toward the house. "Can I help you, sir?"

"What's going on here?" he rasped, angling to get a better view of the inside of the house through the windows.

"Sir, I need to see your ID. How are you related to Ms. Owens?" The officer stepped back with one hand up, gesturing for Blake to stay, while the other hovered over his gun.

Blake knew how cops operated. They functioned similar to the Army, but his mind wasn't processing anything except the crippling fear that gripped him.

He pulled out his wallet and showed his driver's license.

The officer took the ID and shone his flashlight down then back to Blake's face. "Mr. Connor, how are you related to Ms. Owens?" The officer handed his license back.

"I-I'm a neighbor." He pointed in the direction of his house. "And a friend." Without waiting for a response, he moved past the officer, through the open garage door, and into the house. Blake had no doubt the officer had followed, and with his hand still on his weapon.

Blake heard someone else advising stitches were needed as he approached the living room. He took a quick look at Jennifer and sighed in relief.

She's all right. Oh . . . thank you!

All right and mostly in one piece, since it looked as if her bloodied foot was what needed the stitches. He noticed a broken window, too.

"Who are you?" the officer in the living room asked.

"Officer Cortez, this is Captain Blake Connor, Army Ranger," Jennifer said.

Blake raised an eyebrow at her method of establishing his identity, but instead of questioning her, he stared at her foot. "What happened here?"

"Someone broke in, and Ms. Owens stepped on broken glass. Right now, she needs to go to the emergency room to get it looked at." Officer Cortez turned back to Jennifer. "You need to call a relative or a friend so you can stay with them for a night or so. This is not a safe place to stay, with the broken window and all."

Jennifer seemed to hesitate as she looked between Blake and the officer in charge. "I can get a motel room in town."

Blake knew for a fact that she had no relatives close by and jumped in with an absurd idea before he gave it more than a passing thought. This was going to cost him some precious solitary time.

"You'll stay with me, and I'll drive you to the ER now." Blake moved toward Jennifer, and before she could argue, he picked her up from the sofa. His body rebelled at the exertion, but he paid no attention to the discomfort.

"Put me down." She tried to squirm out of his tight hold. "I'm not going to stay at your place."

"Of course you are." He smiled sardonically and glanced over his shoulder. "Officer Cortez, do you mind closing up the house when you're done here? You can reach her at this number." After reciting the digits, Blake ignored Jennifer's repeated protests and walked out of the house and loaded her into the Jeep's passenger seat.

Blake ignored the burning ache from his leg and went back inside the house and hobbled straight into her bedroom. He took a deep breath in an effort to calm his nerves before he started gathering Jennifer's things. He grabbed a few items on the bathroom counter before pulling out several T-shirts, denim jeans, and God, several undergarments from her drawer. He found a duffel bag on the top shelf and shoved everything inside. Picking up the purse on top of the bed, he proceeded outside looking like a man on a mission.

Blake loathed hospitals. After his prolonged confinement in Germany then Walter Reed, he'd vowed to stay away from them every chance he got, but, looking at Jennifer's wound, his resolve flew out the window. He tried driving within the speed limit, but found it impossible. He kept unconsciously pressing the accelerator until he registered the unbelievable speeds of the blurring scenery.

He glanced at Jennifer several times, but found it cumbersome trying to drive with one good eye and keep watch over her at the same time. She hadn't said anything except for the few times he saw her flinching.

"Are you in pain?" His question came out sounding snippier than he had intended. He'd been without company for some time, and he'd forgotten about good manners and tact.

She didn't look at him when she shook her head, but kept staring straight ahead.

Blake ground his molars in frustration.

Why can't she just talk to me?

Because you're an asshole.

What the hell am I supposed to say? I can't do small talk.

You're hopeless.

Irritated with his own voices, he made another attempt with Jennifer. "Look . . . if you're upset because I didn't give you a chance to decide for yourself, it's because I think you needed someone to look after you."

Jennifer whipped her head sideways to glare at him, her mouth thinned in a straight line. "So you assigned *yourself* the task? Thanks, but no thanks. I'm done waiting for you to make good on your word to Trent. Just drop me at the ER, and you can go on your merry way. Hide if you want. I don't care." She went back to staring into the darkness ahead.

Blake was dumbfounded.

The woman had a mouth on her. He felt his anger roar to the surface. Of course, she was right. She'd reached out to him several times and he'd kept her at arm's length. He deserved her brush-off and more.

"As much as I would love to leave you alone, I'm afraid you'll have to endure my presence over the next few days. At least until you get the window fixed and Cortez gives you the go-ahead to return to your house. In the meantime, you're staying with me. It's not a request."

Blake found it nearly impossible not to chuckle as he caught sight of Jennifer's chin jutting forward. Her obvious defiance had him clenching his jaw and struggling to swallow the sound that still escaped as a soft snort.

It had been so long since he'd felt even a semblance of humor that the unfamiliar feeling shocked him. His laughter felt foreign but strangely pleasant.

"I don't enjoy being ordered around, and I don't see what is quite so amusing about my situation. If you're developing a conscience, you can shove it up—" She sighed. "You can forget about it. I don't need your help, or your pity. You know that I have no relatives in town, and you saved me from a lengthy explanation back there. But if you're expecting words of gratitude, you're not getting any." She crossed her arms and huffed.

"Whoa, hold on, little girl. You're using my lines."

They reached the front entrance of the emergency room, and he was prevented from pursuing the subject. He had to concentrate fully on parking near the sliding doors and out of the ambulance bay. Once satisfied, he reached over to release Jennifer's seat belt, accidentally brushing his arm against her breasts. Despite the fabric separating them, he felt his skin burn and jerked in embarrassment.

If Jennifer noticed, she didn't show any sign. "You don't have to treat me like a child. I cut my foot. I'm going to live. There's no need to act like a knight in shining armor." She huffed, sat upright, and swung her legs out the door, clearly indignant and ready to show Blake just how well she could take care of herself.

She froze and Blake smirked, looking over her shoulder at her bare feet.

His eyebrows shot up. "If you want me to stop treating you like a child, then stop acting like one. No reason to risk infection just to show me. Be a good girl, and let me help you."

He picked her up, trying his best to hide his discomfort and keeping his expression as even as possible. His skin felt as though it was going to tear. He walked inside the ER and headed straight to the admitting desk.

The triage nurse looked at them with a surprised expression. "What can I do for you?" she asked, eyeing Jennifer.

"The lady cut her foot. She needs a tetanus shot and some stitches, I believe."

The nurse walked around the desk and unwrapped the bandage that covered Jennifer's foot. After the initial assessment, the nurse returned to her desk, pulled a clipboard, and slipped some papers on it. "I need you to fill out these forms. Have a seat." The nurse gestured toward the sitting area.

Jennifer took the clipboard and squirmed under Blake's grasp. "Put me down, will you?"

Blake gave her a challenging stare and turned back to the nurse. "How long is the wait?" he asked with a tinge of impatience.

"Sir, look around you. See the full room?"

He glanced at the room and muttered, "Not a drop of blood anywhere."

The nurse gave him a stern wave. "We'll call her as soon as we can."

Blake sighed, his displeasure written all over his face. "Thanks."

He walked toward the two empty chairs nearby and deposited Jennifer on one and sat next to her. "Fill out those forms, and I'll take them to the nurse when you're done. Hurry up."

"If you have somewhere to go, you can leave now. As I said, I'll be fine."

"Will you stop shooing me away? Just fill out the damn forms, and be done with it." He tried to calm his brewing temper by taking deep breaths. He crinkled his nose on a deep inhale.

Hospitals had a unique smell—sanitary yet medicinal, in an oddly noxious way—and he absolutely hated them. If he stayed a moment longer, there was a good chance he'd lose it. He stared straight ahead, focusing on the mural across the room.

Raking his eye across the green landscape, he expected a wave of calm to engulf him.

Nothing.

Instead, he felt a rising tension in his shoulders as they pulled toward his ears, bunching up like an angry fist. Resisting the urge to bolt, he started chanting some calming words inside his head.

Jennifer sighed and filled out the forms.

While she took another minute to review them, Blake closed his eyes and tried to block out the incessant reminders of his past as the murmured hum of the other people swirled around him. Blasts of gunfire echoed in his mind, the crying children grated his nerves, and the coughing old man behind him pushed him toward the edge.

"Here," Jennifer said and shoved the clipboard in his hand.

Blake almost shot out of the chair to return the forms to the nurse.

The nurse took the clipboard, inspecting each answer as Blake turned to walk away. "Thanks. We will call her as soon as we can."

Instead of going back to sit with Jennifer, he walked out the ER door. He was better off in the clear air and where he could think. Jennifer had been so close, and the stifling confines of the hospital made him twitchy.

To keep himself occupied, he moved the Jeep to the designated registration parking space and came back to lean against the wall by the entrance.

This turn of events had surprised him.

Lancaster was generally a safe place to live. Reported burglaries were few, but with the influx of new faces moving into the once sleepy town, there could be no guarantee what type of characters were in their midst anymore.

After what seemed like forever, he saw a nurse through the glass door approaching Jennifer with a wheelchair. Debating whether or not to join her, he watched Jennifer wince as she eased into the chair with the nurse's help. As much as he wanted to leave, a sudden attack of guilt had him stepping on the pad and waiting for the glass doors to open so he could follow the direction he'd seen them wheel Jennifer.

The flimsy cubicle curtain was all that was between him and hearing everything happening on the other side.

He waited outside, trying his best to appear inconspicuous.

An eye patch and a beanie in the middle of this heatwave . . . fat chance no one will notice me.

Sure enough, several nurses passing by glanced his way and were quick to look away.

Blake stayed glued to his spot during the arduous wait. He heard Jennifer gasp and the doctor chastise her while suturing her instep.

After announcing six stitches were firmly in place, advising Jennifer to stay off her feet for a week—no driving either—the doctor walked out of the small cubicle and was taken aback when he saw Blake standing outside. "Can I help you?"

Blake shook his head. "I'm Ms. Owens' ride."

"She's inside. You can go in." The doctor pulled the curtain open for him.

Blake hesitated. One look at the miserable expression on Jennifer's face and he almost stumbled in his haste to get to her. "What's wrong? How are you feeling? Are you okay? What do you need? Should I call the doctor back?" He felt a cold finger of fear tickle his spine as the words spilled out in a rush, and he brushed the tendrils of hair that fell over her face.

"I won't be able to move around for a week, and I can't even drive." Her voice was low, filled with dread and something else he couldn't pinpoint.

Without considering what she thought of him, he stepped closer, tilted her chin up and stared into her eyes. "Don't worry about the things you can't control. Just follow the doctor's orders, and stay off that foot."

It might have been the pain from the cut, the shock of finding her house turned upside down, or the fear of losing control that pushed Jennifer to tears, Blake would never know, but compassion dictated his next move. He wrapped his arms around her and pulled her head against his chest. The comfort was meant for her, but he felt a different kind of emotion, something he hadn't felt before. For the first time in a long time, the ache he felt was not his own. At that moment, he wanted nothing more than the power to ease her pain and all that troubled her.

—⁓—

Jennifer surrendered to the warmth of Blake's embrace, savoring human contact that she'd been denied since Trent's demise. She had forgotten how much she enjoyed physical connection. The pain of the past, the loss of loved ones, and the uncertainty of her future all hit her at once, and Blake held her as the worst of her emotions broke out in torrents.

He said nothing. Instead, he continued holding her until the last of her tears had ebbed.

She had no idea how much time had passed while each of them clung to the other, but she was jerked back to the present when she heard someone clear his throat.

Blake let her go and took her hand.

The doctor held up a pair of aluminum crutches and a prescription. "This should help you get around, but as I said before, you'll need to stay off that foot for at least a week. I'd hate to see you back here again with open sutures. The prescription is for pain. It might knock you out in the beginning, but it'll do its job. The sutures will have to be checked by either your regular doctor or come back here after seven days. If your wound is healing as expected, then the sutures can be removed at that time."

Jennifer watched the doctor in a daze.

Blake must have sensed her helplessness and took over. "I'll make sure she's off her feet. Anything else, doctor?"

"I believe we're done here. Remember, no dancing and no strenuous activities until the wound is healed."

Blake chuckled and Jennifer blinked at the double entendre. "I don't dance so I'm pretty sure she won't either." Blake took the crutches from the doctor and handed them to her. "Here, why don't you see if you can manage to walk with them?"

She hopped off the examination table and fitted the crutches in her armpits. She took a few steps but felt her balance go as the rubber end slid one way and her body went the other.

Blake grabbed her by the waist to steady her.

She gritted her teeth. "This is not going to be easy."

Blake gathered her purse and walked out of the room. "Shall we?"

With slow, ungainly steps and heavy heart, Jennifer followed him out of the emergency room and into the quiet night. She was out of her element. Several emotions warred inside her, mingling with the pain from the newly sutured wound. The uncertainty of the coming week and the remnants of Blake's embrace tangled within, making her want to run away for sheer self-preservation.

With nothing but the car radio playing softly in the background, Blake seemed wrapped up in his thoughts and left her to her own devices.

Jennifer had no problem with the companionable silence. It gave her the chance to think.

How in God's name did I end up here?

Coleen had been successful in planting a seed of doubt at lunch regarding Blake, and Jennifer could stop searching for reasons why had he moved in the same town.

Once they reached his house, Blake parked the Jeep on the driveway.

She noticed that his movement had markedly slowed as soon as he stepped out of the vehicle.

He pulled out Jennifer's duffel from the backseat and winced.

Jennifer hopped out of the vehicle and tried to keep up with him on the gravel walkway. "What's wrong?" she asked, trying not to sound worried.

"Nothing."

In the glow of the moonlight, she saw the hard line on his face. The walls were up once again, and she knew prying further would get her nowhere.

He opened the door and turned the light on. "I'll set you up in my bedroom, and I'll take the couch in the extra room."

Jennifer glanced around the living room and stopped in her tracks. "No, I'll only be here for one night. There's no need for you to give up your bed. I'll sleep in the extra room."

He whipped around and gave her an agonized stare. "Jennifer, please. I want you to be comfortable. A couch isn't ideal for someone who's nursing an injury."

Her heart ached at the look on his face and sound of his voice, but she couldn't let it go. "And you're not? Look at you . . . you exerted yourself tonight. Don't bother arguing with me. I can see it in your face."

His chin lifted in that proud manner she was beginning to recognize. She could see that her words had cut through him, but he didn't deny them.

"I'm going to my therapy tomorrow. Sam will ease the tightness. Please, do this for me. Use my bedroom for the duration of your stay here. Don't argue. It's late, and I'm tired."

As much as she wanted to pursue the subject, she knew what it had taken for him to admit to being tired.

"Fine . . . I'll use your room tonight, but I'm out of here tomorrow."

A glint of triumph flickered in his eye before he turned and led her to his room. "Let's take it day by day," he said.

Everything about his bedroom screamed masculine simplicity—from the heady scent that assaulted her to the muted color of his bedspread and the sparse furniture. No clutter, just the basics. A digital clock sat on a nightstand, a lamp and a desk occupied the opposite end of the room, and mountains of *Playboy* magazines piled beside the bed.

An unexpected grin eased across his face as Blake realized what she'd spotted, but he simply shrugged and offered no excuses. He placed her duffel bag next to the bed. "I'll get a towel for you. Remember, you can't wet your feet yet, so I suggest a sponge bath." The humorous lilt of his voice was unmistakable.

Jennifer sat on the bed and rested the crutches next to her. She hoped her jaw wasn't as far on the floor as she thought it might be.

She ignored his jibe. "Thanks."

"I'll be in the room across the hallway."

She let out a sigh and tried to relax. It had been a long day.

Blake came back after a few minutes with a towel and placed it on the bed next to her. He stood close with hands in his pocket. "I'm glad nothing happened to you. It could've been worse. Now, try to get some sleep. If you need anything, I'll leave my door open so I can hear you." He brushed an errant wisp of hair away from her face.

Jennifer's breath stilled, reminded of the tender gesture in the hospital. "Thanks," she said softly.

——◊◊◊——

Sometime before dawn, Jennifer sat upright with heart pounding and unsure why. It took a minute for her to recognize her surroundings. She heard a hoarse cry coming from somewhere in the hallway.

Blake.

She fumbled out of bed. Her foot throbbed the moment she lowered her legs to the floor. She had forgotten where she'd left the crutches and rather than looking for them, she hopped on her good foot into the darkness and toward the sound.

Ignoring the pain radiating up her leg, she limped into the other room, and knelt down beside the couch. Jennifer placed a hand on his arm and gently nudged him.

Blake continued mumbling. His skin was sweaty to the touch.

She moved her hand to his shoulder and gave a vigorous shake. "Blake," she whispered.

It took several shakes, but his eyes snapped open, and he grabbed her arm and twisted—hard.

"Ow! Blake, it's me, Jennifer! You're having a nightmare."

It took several seconds for the bright sand hill to fade into the darkened drywall of the familiar spare room, and even longer for Blake to loosen his grip on his M16 rifle and watch Jennifer slump to the floor.

She was gasping and looking plain scared.

"Jennifer, what are you doing here?" He shot off the couch in such a hurry that his skin burned at the sudden movement. He bellowed and contracted into a ball.

Spasticity was often taken for granted, and he kept forgetting that abrupt movements tended to stretch his skin beyond its limits. It was a sharp reminder that he had to stop foregoing his occupational therapy sessions.

Jennifer scrambled to her feet, using the couch as her crutch. "You were having a nightmare. I heard you from the bedroom."

He saw her wide eyes and pale skin reflecting the faint glow of the nightlight. "Did I hurt you?"

"No, you just scared the hell out of me when you pulled that Steven Segal move." She sat down on the edge of the sofa and slowed her breathing. "What's going on, Blake? Is there anything I can do for you?"

Blake shook his head and crossed the room to turn on the lights. "Go back to your room, Jennifer."

Jennifer squinted and, ignoring his order, asked, "What's wrong? I'm sure it's not all about counting sheep that caused the nightmare. Care to talk about it?"

Her concern caused his defensive wall to slam firmly into place. He'd rather not deal with compassion and tenderness. He despised being weak and helpless, and Jennifer's voice was packed with healthy doses of the unwanted sympathy.

"I didn't know you were a shrink. Not that I ever needed one."

"C'mon, Blake, even big boys like you need to unload."

He settled on the opposite end of the couch, wincing as he spread his legs in front of him. "You want me to talk about the horrors of war? You want to hear the gory details of staring into my dead comrades' eyes seconds after I pulled them to safety?"

Her eyes widened. "Is that what happened to Trent?"

"I wasn't talking about Trent." He rammed his fingers through his hair in disgust. "You have no idea what I've seen out there."

"You can talk about what you've seen out there with me, Blake. If that's what it'd take to get the load off your chest." Her tone was low and calm. She scooted closer on the couch.

Too damn close.

With unfathomable weariness, he shook his head. "I'm not going to burden you with the horrors of combat. Those are the details I take to my grave."

She reached out her hand, and he jerked away. "If talking won't help, maybe I can ease some of the pain in your arms." She reached for his hand again.

It took a tremendous amount of self-control not to pull his hand away. The softness of her skin against his made him tingle. Her touch alone elicited a sleeping urge within him, and he tried to curb the unwanted response.

"That feels so good." He moaned, unable to resist and too exhausted to try any longer.

His words seemed to embolden her, and Jennifer moved her hand past his wrist and up his arm, pushing up the sleeve of his cotton shirt. The sensation eased the prickling in his contracted skin.

Blake closed his eyes, savoring every second of her touch. Encountering his rough, scarred limb didn't seem to deter Jennifer as she skimmed her deft fingers over his hand.

"What else can I do for you?"

Her hands massaged the raised scars and eased the tension in his rigid muscles while her question took him beyond the physical and reached deep into his soul. Blake opened his good eye, reached out, and tilted her chin up. "You've done more than you'll ever know." He focused on her mouth.

When her tongue darted between her lips as if anticipating him, he gave in to the irresistible urge, lowering his mouth over hers. Tentative at first, but when she offered no resistance, he increased the pressure and let the softness of her kiss guide him. He felt a spark zip though his body, reaching his toes and they separated as though reaching for more of it. His heart seemed to stop and jump-start at the same time. The world stopped and his mind raced, and nothing else seemed to matter as he slipped his tongue into the warmth of her parted lips.

Jennifer shuddered, and he pressed his body even closer.

Heaven.

She was everything Blake had expected her to be and more. Her feminine scent wafted through his nostrils, inviting him to take more of her.

She responded by deepening the kiss, and the electric pulses doubled throughout his body, transforming into a throbbing delight that he'd almost forgotten he could feel. It was impossible to think straight.

Jennifer wound her hands around his neck, and he applied pressure on her back by pulling her close until her breasts rubbed his chest.

He wound his fingers through the silky strands of her hair and loved the way her body molded into his.

Endless moments seemed to have passed before he found the strength to ease away from her. He tilted his head away and pressed his mouth into the side of his arm until he knew he could take looking at her again. "I'm so sorry. I shouldn't have kissed you."

Jennifer searched his face as if she would find the reason for this madness written there.

Without giving her a chance to respond, he moved to the door. "Go back to your bedroom and lock the door," he said, his voice low, almost pleading as he stepped into the darkness without ever looking back.

———

Jennifer remained unmoving. She stared at the door wondering what had happened. Things happened so fast, and she had simply reacted.

Did I want that, too?

She felt heat flush across her face.

Damn right, you did.

She would've continued kissing him if he hadn't stopped. There was no lying about it, at least not to herself.

Shame and guilt settled as the truth seeped in.

What have I done?

She traced a finger along her lips, mesmerized with the tingle still lingering there as the memory of its source replayed behind her closed eyes. She pushed off the couch and, on one good but shaky leg, hopped back into Blake's bedroom.

The hallway light was off, and she had no idea where he'd gone.

She closed the door but left it unlocked. She took three ibuprofen pills and exhaustion claimed her after a few minutes. Her remaining thoughts were all about Blake . . . and the kiss.

When Jennifer awoke the next morning, her first conscious thought was of Blake. She rolled over and gazed out the window overlooking the patio, only to realize the glare streaming through the gap in the blinds meant it was late in the day, and she'd overslept.

She sat up and checked the clock. It was almost ten in the morning.

Good heavens! Must've been the pain pills.

As if on cue, her foot began to throb.

She searched for any sign of bleeding but saw nothing except the dried remnants that had stained the cloth. She found her crutches perched by the wall next to the nightstand, and with a few hops, she fitted the crutches in her armpits and stabilized her weight on her hands.

Thanks to Blake's thoughtfulness, all her stuff had been packed as if she'd done it herself. She dressed in a pair of denim shorts and comfortable T-shirt.

The house was almost too quiet except for a scratching sound coming from the living room.

She found Blake's dog perched on the sofa, looking out the window.

Drew spun around, and if dogs could smile, she would have sworn he was greeting her with a big good morning grin. He looked grateful, almost relieved, for the company. He'd seen her once yet seemed comfortable and not showing any aggression toward her. The powerful-looking animal approached her, his tongue lolled out.

"Hey, Drew. You aren't surprised to see me at all, are you?" She reached down and patted him on the head. "Where's Blake?"

The dog's ears perked up when he heard his master's name, and he glanced back at the window.

"So that's what you were doing . . . waiting for him?"

Jennifer was surprised when Drew rose up on his hind legs and rested his paws on her chest, almost knocking her off balance.

She giggled. "You must be good company for Blake." She patted his head again and turned in the direction of the kitchen.

Although Blake hadn't shown her around, it wasn't hard to guess since the layout of the house seemed to be similar to hers. Besides, all she had to do was to follow the scent of freshly brewed coffee. With care, she hobbled into the adjoining room and found a mug sitting next to the coffee maker.

After pouring a cup for herself, Jennifer sat at the dinette and took stock of her surroundings in the light of day. She had no idea how he lived, but judging by the limited provisions around her, Blake seemed to be a simple man.

The memory of their kiss surfaced, and another wave of shame filled her. She had acted on impulse when she'd returned his kiss, but had he not pushed her away, and stopping had been the last thing in her mind.

Jennifer intended to have him drive her home as soon as he appeared. If the prospect of limping outside on a crutch in this heat didn't make her break out in an exhausted sweat, she would have started the long walk home now.

Halfway through her first cup, the telephone rang. She debated whether to answer the call, but Blake had given Officer Cortez the number in case he had news about the break-in.

As soon as she picked up the receiver, a reprimanding female voice lashed out. "Blake Connor, didn't I teach you better manners? You should be ashamed of yourself, letting your poor mother worry about you."

Jennifer pulled the phone away and stared at it.

Should I say something or just hang up?

Her good manners prevailed. "Hello? I'm sorry, but Blake isn't home at the moment." She cringed at the sound of her voice.

"Oh . . . I'm so sorry."

Jennifer gripped the phone and struggled for the right thing to fill the silence.

It's okay, Mrs. Connor. I'm not just some random woman . . . here . . . at your son's home . . . first thing in the morning . . . well, I am, but . . . I'm just a friend.

Oh yeah, sounds great!

"I'm Claire, Blake's mother. Who am I speaking with?"

"Um, I-I-I'm Jennifer . . . Jennifer Owens, Mrs. Connor. My house was burglarized last night and I'm a neighbor and I cut my foot on a broken vase and Blake offered for me to stay for the night while I get my window fixed." She leaned on the wall to support her body and tried to catch her breath.

"Oh my! Are you okay?" The pure concern in Mrs. Connor's voice made Jennifer ache for her own mother.

"Yes. Blake took me to the ER last night, and I'm waiting for a call from the police department to see if they have any information on the burglar."

"Blake did? Bless his heart. I'm glad he's making friends. He has been cooped up for too long. It's about time he mingled."

Long time?

"Exactly how long ago was he injured?"

"Um . . . let's see . . . I'd say almost a year ago. I know a close friend died in the blast, and he hasn't spoken about him. I only found out some of the details when he was given the award. He doesn't want to talk about it. I understand his reluctance, though. I'm sure it must be painful for him."

"He's been living here for that long?" She couldn't stop herself from asking.

"Yes, he insisted on moving there. His father and I had our doubts, you know. We weren't sure he was fit enough to be on his own, considering his injuries, but Blake has never been one to be deterred once he sets his mind. I worry about him. He's not very cooperative with the therapy, and that woman, Katrina, didn't help matters at all. If I ever see her again, I'll happily give her a piece of my mind. Humph!"

"I'm sorry. *Katrina?*"

"Oh, my. I've said more than I should. It's been nice talking to you, Jennifer. Please ask my son to give his mother a call once he gets in." She laughed. "We're going to visit soon. I would love if we could meet."

"That would be nice, Mrs. Connor. I'll give Blake the message." Jennifer was surprised to hear the words as they came out of her mouth, but something about Blake's mother put her at ease. She was easy to talk to, and better yet, she offered up so much about Blake, making any prying on Jennifer's part completely unnecessary.

Jennifer pondered the new information about Blake. Were his injuries connected to Trent's death? What about the medal his mother had mentioned? If he had been living in Lancaster for almost a year . . .

All this time he's been keeping his promise to Trent.

A wave of guilt washed over her.

Jennifer had just poured her second cup of coffee when she heard the front door open and close.

Drew bounded toward the living room, his eager bark filling the entire house.

Blake walked into the kitchen. He wore a white long-sleeve cotton T-shirt, jeans, a camouflage beanie, and a grim expression on his face.

Last night's kiss popped into Jennifer's mind, and she tried to push the thoughts away. Plastering a smile on her face, she rose from her chair to get a cup for him.

"Sit down. I want to talk to you." His mouth tightened into a straight line while he waited for her. "I swung by the precinct on my way home and spoke with Officer Cortez. He still hasn't ID'd the burglar, and he wants me to tell you it's not safe for you to return to your place until you're able to protect yourself."

Jennifer sighed. "I can't possibly put you out longer. I can get a room at the motel—"

"Will you stop with that already? You're here, and this is where you'll stay until the cops say it's safe for you to go back to your house. Look at the way you hobble around. You can barely do for yourself. With that bum foot, you can't drive, which means no groceries, no work, nothing. You really don't have much option." His tone infuriated her, so superior, but his arguments made a lot of sense, even if she didn't want to hear them.

Jennifer closed her eyes. She was going to be at Blake's mercy for several more days. There was no way around it. She wasn't sure if that was what really bothered her, or if it was the fact he had the power to make her respond.

"If you're worried about staying longer because I might kiss you again, you can rest easy. That was a mistake, and it won't happen again."

Her mouth dropped open for a moment before she snapped it shut and stared at him in disgust.

"It's settled then. Now, if you'll give me the keys to your house, I'll get some more clothes for you. I'll bring your briefcase and your laptop, too, so you can work." He spoke in a matter-of-fact tone.

"My laptop and briefcase are in the car," she said.

"Where are your car keys?"

Oh, you condescending ass!

"What's your problem, Blake?" she asked.

"I don't have a problem." He walked out of the room, leaving her seething in frustration.

Jennifer rose from the chair and hobbled to follow him. She found him sitting on the sofa in the living room. "If you want me to stay here for a few more days, you have to make some major attitude adjustments. You're not exactly good company."

"Don't worry about my manners. I'll make sure to stay out of your way. Now, get your keys so I can pick up your things. If you have any other items you want me to bring, now's the time to tell me."

"You're an impossible man," Jennifer said, and moved out of the living room with as much dignity as she could muster. She stayed in the bedroom, refusing to go out and face Blake until she was certain she could control her temper.

Obnoxious and irritating and acting like I haven't been taking care of myself since . . .

He makes a pretty darn good argument.

Yeah, okay, maybe, but his approach is too bossy. Who does he think he is?

Trent's best friend?

That doesn't mean he gets to run my life and order me around.

A few hours later, hunger forced an end to her mental debate, and she decided to come out of the bedroom.

Jennifer found Blake on the sofa, staring at the television. He didn't even look up when she walked by.

Drew trotted behind her.

Might as well make myself handy.

She smiled and rubbed the dog's ears, unable to hold on to her anger when he nuzzled her hand. "Let's see what we can rustle up for lunch, Drew. I'm sure your master is hungry by now." She opened the freezer. Except for ice trays, there was nothing but cold air blasting her in the face. "Does he even eat?" she asked the dog.

When his head tilted sideways, she giggled.

"Yes, I do."

Jennifer gasped, whipping around to face the door.

"I just haven't gotten the chance to pick up some stuff. If you're hungry, I'm calling for pizza. Write down what you want from the store, and I'll pick them up when I swing by your house this afternoon," Blake said. His mouth was still set in a grim line, but his tone lacked the sting it had held earlier.

Her stomach answered first with a growl loud enough for Blake to hear. She blushed but sighed in relief when he grinned. "Pizza sounds good to me."

He walked toward the phone and picked up the receiver. "What do you want on it?"

"Hawaiian sounds good right now, but I'm okay if you want something else." She sat on the chair and studied him.

The right side of his face seemed to have escaped injury. Every visible inch of skin was smooth and healthy looking. The left side, however, was another thing. Raised scars and shiny skin were still healing. She knew how painful her own minor burns had been in the past, and the thought made her heart lurch at the vision of his suffering.

At that same moment, Blake glanced in her direction and caught her watching. His expression immediately soured. He turned around and finished his pizza order, sounding angry.

Blake slammed the phone down and stormed out of the kitchen, leaving her at a loss.

What the . . .

His mood swings were giving her whiplash. If she hadn't known his kind and easygoing manner before, she never would have believed it. His temper was enough to make her dream of escape. What a pity.

She decided the best way to improve their relationship for the time being was to give him what he wanted. She started the grocery list, as well as a list of the things she needed from her place.

She had no idea what the man liked or if he even ate, despite what he'd said. She could make the usual meatloaf, pasta, and chicken salad that Trent had loved so much. Recalling the picture she had of him with Trent, Blake had lost a tremendous amount of weight. He wasn't thin, but the man could use ten more pounds.

After finishing both lists, Jennifer found Blake sitting outside on the front porch. She took a deep, steady breath.

Try harder, girl. It's only fair.

"Here is the key to my house, and I need this prescription filled," she said, settling down next to him on one of the porch chairs. She saw a glint of amusement flicker across his face when he took the key.

His mouth twitched into something resembling a smile.

"Oh! Your mother called. She wanted me to tell you that she's expecting you to call her when you get back. I forgot to mention it right away."

He appeared startled. "You spoke with her?"

"Yes, I answered thinking it might be Officer Cortez."

"What else did she say?"

Jennifer decided to tell him the truth. "Your mom wants to meet me. She said they'll be dropping by soon."

Blake slapped his forehead, leaned back against his seat, and didn't say another word.

When the pizza arrived, they spent the entire time eating in silence.

Well, no conversation is better than biting each other's head off, I suppose.

Jennifer hadn't expected to oversleep again. She wasn't sure what it was about being under this roof that made her sleep longer than usual. She was typically an early riser and could count on one hand the number of times she woke later than six.

It has to be the meds.

Her immediate thoughts turned to Blake. True to his words, he had come back from her place with all the things she needed. He hadn't said anything apart from good night when he'd retreated to the other room, leaving her alone in the quiet house.

She sat up, and pain radiated from her injured foot. The doctor hadn't been joking when he'd warned her that healing would take longer than she wanted. Gingerly planting her good foot on the wooden floor, she pushed her body off the bed and hopped to the bathroom.

She was limping out of the bathroom when she heard dishes clattering. It sounded as though Blake had beaten her to the cooking duties this morning. The scent of bacon drifted into the hallway, while the aroma of coffee invited her to join him. She placed most of her weight on the good foot and hopped toward the kitchen.

Blake looked up and his lips turned into a grim line when their eyes met.

He was wearing a navy cotton T-shirt that covered an incongruous looking vest and dark jeans.

Swallowing the cheerful greeting, she braced herself for an onslaught.

"What the hell are you doing walking around without your crutches?" he asked, striding to her side in a few quick steps. Without a word, he pulled her off her feet and carried her to the waiting chair.

Here we go.

"Good morning to you, too. And I'm not walking on it." She felt like a child.

A smile and a hello really too much to ask for?

"You're an adult and shouldn't need to be reminded what's good for you and what isn't," he said, before he returned his attention to the stove.

"I know what my body is capable of doing, so don't worry about me," she answered.

Blake pivoted and threw her a dagger glare, which she returned in defiance.

"Then use that brain of yours."

She seethed but decided it wasn't worth the argument. "Someone woke up on the wrong side of the bed."

Blake's shoulder muscles tensed and his nostrils flared, but he didn't answer.

Aha! Stand up for myself, and he backs down. Hello, weak spot.

The silence was disconcerting, but again, better than getting into another disagreement. Jennifer took a deep breath and closed her eyes.

"Eat everything. I swear, you're like a stick. You need some meat on you." He deposited the plate filled with bacon, eggs, and toast as well as a steaming cup of coffee in front of her.

"I'm not thin."

"Whatever. Just eat."

"What about you?" she asked, eyeing the food on the plate, and her stomach grumbled in anticipation.

"I'm going out." He didn't even look at her. Instead, he grabbed the keys, whistled for the dog, and walked out the door before she could think of a reply.

Fuming, she turned to the food and stuffed her face while she plotted ways not just out of this house but out of his life as well.

I'm better off on my own.

There was more going on with this man than what she saw on the surface. Anger, resentment, and something she couldn't quite put her finger on. She had known him to be an incredible friend to Trent and fun to be around. He had been a pleasant man the little time she'd been around him with Trent. So what had turned him into this bitter person? Was it the war and death he'd seen? If he was that broken, then she wasn't equipped to fix him. This shattered man was beyond help.

After the dishes were done, she went back to the bedroom and made several phone calls. Her first was to Mr. Smith, her elderly neighbor and friend of Aunt Debbie's.

While she listened to the ringing, she glanced around Blake's room and the pile of magazines caught her attention again. The all-too-male reading material made her blush as she pictured Blake smothering her body with kisses. She had never thought of herself as a prude, but her imagination had been getting the best of her.

Not good.

"Hello?" Mr. Smith's baritone was so comfortably familiar and reminded her of home.

"Hi, it's Jennifer. I'm sure you heard about the break-in by now."

"Child, I was so worried. I came by yesterday morning to check on you. How are you?"

"I'm sorry. I forgot to call you right away. I'm all right. I had to go to the ER to get stitched up, but I'm okay. I'm staying at a friend's house until I can get the house fixed."

"A friend?" Mr. Smith sounded doubtful. He knew that she had no friends in the area. It was one reason for the frequent invitations from him and his wife for holiday meals.

"Yes . . ." She didn't want to get into the details. "I have a favor to ask."

"Sure, name it."

"I need help getting the broken window replaced. I was wondering if you—"

"You got it."

Jennifer smiled. "I will schedule everything and have the company call you when they are ready to drop by for measurements and installation."

"Just give them my number, and I'll take care of the rest." His voice softened. "I'm sorry this happened to you. If there's anything we can do, please let us know."

After they hung up, she placed a call to Officer Cortez. There were no new developments, but he assured her that they were doing their best to find answers for her. With a promise of an update, they ended the call.

Her last call was to the window company. The earliest they could do the job was in a few days, which was good enough for her. She could brave out a couple of days in her own house. It was better than enduring Blake's endlessly impossible mood swings. That was what she kept telling herself, trying not to think of the kiss.

Blake had no idea how long he'd been driving around until exhaustion got the best of him. He parked along the shoulder of the empty highway to clear his mind. After all, he was not back to his usual self yet. His stamina wasn't what it used to be, and his body always found a way to subdue him into submitting to its limits.

Rewinding his memories to earlier in the day, Blake wasn't proud of his outburst. He was unraveling in front of this woman faster than his mind could even process. Sure, he'd had a valid argument, but he wasn't the best authority on good behavior. He couldn't even follow Sam's instruction on how to properly care for his injuries.

He pounded on the steering wheel in frustration.

What a hypocrite!

Drew yelped from the backseat.

He patted the dog's head and went back to his thoughts. As of late, he'd become his own worst enemy and Jennifer's presence had had a remarkable effect on his roller coaster of emotions. One second, he was a jackass biting her head off, and the next, he wanted to protect her from anything and everyone, including himself.

He wished he no longer harbored feelings for her, and feared another moment with her would make him transparent to the point of exposing her effect on him. Her touches made him realize that he needed a woman in his life. Sure, he could pay a whore to satisfy his needs and give him the much-needed jerk off, but would that fulfill his yearning?

Man, this is getting complicated.

He cranked the Jeep and checked for any oncoming traffic before easing onto the highway and driving straight to the rehab center.

After he parked, he pulled his cell phone from his pocket and autodialed his home number. Four rings and his answering machine picked up. Feeling a bit silly, he left a quick message before he lost his nerve, hoping that Jennifer might be listening.

"Jennifer, I know I acted like an ass again this morning. I apologize for that. It's just . . . man, this is hard for me. I don't want you hurting yourself. If you need anything while I'm out, you can call me on my cell phone." He left his number and hung up.

I'm pathetic.

"C'mon, boy." He whistled the moment he slipped out of the driver's seat.

The dog jumped down and was at his side within a few seconds.

He attached the leash to Drew's collar before they made their way to his appointment.

"Well, this is a pleasant surprise," Sam said as the pair came through the door.

"I'm here, so get over it," Blake said, feeling glum.

A grin spread across his buddy's face, and he met Blake at the workout table. "And you are wearing your vest, too. This is amazing. I wonder which god I have to thank for this breakthrough."

Blake wasn't in the mood for the jerk's teasing. He grunted and sat on the table to wait.

"Fine, do your thing. But I want you to know that I'm proud of you for taking the first step into looking after yourself."

"Yada yada." Blake tuned him out, not interested in hearing the pep talk about the benefits of wearing the damn vest.

The contraption was heavy, not to mention uncomfortable and hot. He only had it on because, even though he hated to admit it, he felt better wearing the darn thing.

"Remove your shirt and the vest. I want to check the skin's healing progress," Sam said, breaking into his self-imposed cocoon.

Blake yanked his shirt off but faltered when it came to the vest. Even though Sam had seen his ghastly looking body, the idea remained unnerving. He hesitated, his fingers locking stiff.

"Man, let's not make this a big deal. I've seen worse." Sam's tone was gentle yet firm enough to show he meant business.

Damn Sam for reading him like an open book. Slowly, Blake removed the Velcro strap that held the vest in place and dropped the garment on the floor. He flopped on the table to let Sam do his thing and closed his eyes, not wanting to see the man's reaction to the repulsive sight before him. Instead, he listened to Sam's tennis shoes squeaking across the floor while he inspected him like a piece of meat.

Blake let out a long sigh, showing his impatience at the process. "What?" he asked, unable to stand the silence any longer.

"You have left the burns to heal on their own, and although they've healed well enough, I can see contractures on some. Do you feel like you can't move your body at a certain angles?" Sam's tone somehow planted another layer on his already rotten pile of doubts.

"Sometimes." His answer was short and clipped. He didn't want to add insecurity to his growing list of unspoken fears, but he knew he was screwed and there wasn't much he could do about it.

"It has been almost a year, right?"

Blake clenched his jaw and kept all the rude comebacks he had to himself.

"There's a little irritation right here." Sam touched the area, and Blake flinched.

"So?"

"I'm going to phone Dr. McCall and schedule an appointment for you. It's a simple debridement. Other than that, you're doing well. Keep wearing the vest. No matter how worthless you think it is, it's doing its job."

Blake said nothing when Sam stepped out of the room. He lay on his stomach and spread his arms above his head to relax, easing the stiffness in his joints.

He was dozing by the time Sam returned and started rotation exercises followed by extensions and flexes. The session went by fast, and he felt much better than when he'd first come in.

"I'll pick you up tonight at eight. And I won't take no for an answer this time," Sam said and strode off to another waiting patient before Blake could respond.

Whatever.

Sam was going to learn that Blake couldn't be ordered around, even if it was for his own good.

Blake put on his vest and then his shirt, and left without saying a word. That was the perk of having Drew around. There was no need for any conversation.

On a whim, he stopped by the grocery store and picked up some steaks as a sort of peace offering. Words might not be sufficient, but maybe his actions could redeem him. Blake vowed to make a conscious effort to avoid snapping at Jennifer.

I can do this. Piece of cake.

He had to try, at least, even if her closeness was killing him.

—⁓—

Jennifer was packing her bag when the phone rang, and she let the machine pick up. The last thing she needed was another conversation with his mother, even if she meant well. She liked the woman, even if their chat had been brief, but there was little point in forging any friendship with a woman she would never meet.

She had an idea how Blake had gotten injured from the bits and pieces she had gathered from the conversation with his mother and Colonel Norwalk. She was certain it was connected to Trent's death, but broaching the subject might send him into a tailspin. It would be nice to get the old Blake back, the charismatic and tenderhearted man she once knew. This new Blake seemed hell-bent on ignoring his needs. And that was something she had to ignore, too. As much as she wanted to help, the man had deep-seated issues way beyond what she was capable of understanding. He was a classic example of the returning soldiers who had seen the bitter effects of war, and she was out of her element around him. What he needed was professional help and a healthy dose of understanding. If only he would open up, it might make it easier for her to get through to him.

Her heart constricted when Blake's voice drifted from the little speaker. While sweet, his apology wasn't what she needed. His moods and outbursts were difficult to handle, but not as difficult as the attraction she felt for him. She had enough troubles. Allowing him in any further had disaster written all over. She still found herself storing his cell number on her phone.

Not that I'm going to call, but . . . it can't hurt to have it.

After clearing her things as fast as she could manage, Jennifer took one last look around his bedroom and departed. She decided against leaving a note. That seemed a bit melodramatic, and she wasn't up for darkening her already cloudy mood.

Shoeless on her injured foot, Jennifer tried to hobble on her good one with the aid of the crutches. She looked at the distance she had to cover. The pavement was hot, and it didn't help that her bag was heavy, yet she took each step like a trooper.

What should have been a ten-minute walk took four times longer. By the time she had reached her front step, she was tired, sweaty, and in pain. It took her a moment to muster enough courage to enter her own house.

She crossed the threshold, hoping for peace and quiet, away from everything that Blake stirred within her, but she couldn't stop the small shivers that kept running through her. She'd been told it was natural to feel wary after a break-in, that a violated space had a way of making a person jittery.

She took a deep breath and locked the door behind her, engaging the chain for an added sense of false security. She hobbled to her bedroom and dropped the heavy bag on the chair. Without skipping a beat, she rummaged through her purse for the pill bottle and popped one inside her mouth.

Jennifer limped to the shower, turned on the water, and stripped out of her sweaty clothes. She took one look at her foot and gasped. The bandage was soaked with blood.

Not good.

She lifted the gauze, and upon closer inspection, she saw that she'd popped a couple of stitches. She took a quick shower and cleansed the site afterward. By the time she was done, the pain meds had kicked in, and she went to bed, welcoming the shelter of sleep.

It was past midnight when she awoke, feeling disoriented and on the verge of panic. She listened in the darkness for sounds, anything that would justify her stupidity in leaving the safety of Blake's house. Her immediate surroundings were quiet, but the fear inside her wouldn't go away. The broken window hadn't been replaced yet, and she knew she was as vulnerable as if she was standing outside unprotected. The fear that gripped her was crippling, leaving her in tears and unable to rationalize her thoughts.

Unless she called the cops, she had no one to come to her aid. Mr. Smith was much too old to be disturbed at this unholy hour.

I can call—

No! Get a grip, Jennifer.

Swallowing the lump in her throat, she shook her head, grabbed her cell phone off the table, and dialed Blake's number.

The phone rang several times before an unfamiliar voice picked up.

She almost hung up, but then she heard the magic words.

"This is Blake's cell. How can I help you?"

She hesitated for a moment before she found the courage to speak up. "Can I speak with Blake, please?"

There was a rustling in the background as if a phone was exchanging hands.

"Yesh?" Blake slurred the word.

"Blake, it's Jennifer. I'm scared. I'm at home. Can you please pick me up?" She swallowed the scream stuck in her throat when a noise sounded just outside her bedroom window.

"Jenny?"

Her heart skipped. Blake was the only person who had ever called her Jenny and only when he was being playful.

"Yeah, it's me. Can you please pick me up?"

"I'm coming to get you right . . . now. Sam, let's go to Jenny . . . she needs me."

Jennifer heard a click, and the line disconnected. She made as little noise as possible as she rushed out of bed, completely forgetting about her bandaged foot. Yelping in pain, she didn't waste a minute gathering the bag she had left in the chair and huddled beside the door to wait in the darkness.

The doorbell chimed.

Oh, thank God!

She opened the door to find a man she had never seen before. The scream she had forced down minutes before rushed to her lips, and she dropped everything, fully prepared to bolt in the opposite direction in hopes she could reach the phone before the strange man managed to grab her.

"Jennifer, wait. I'm Sam. Blake's in the car."

The hurried explanation halted her. "Sam? What happened to Blake?"

"I'll explain in the car. Blake wants you out of here."

Jennifer, with a little help from Sam, managed to get out to the car.

"Take the backseat with him," Sam said, climbing behind the wheel and revving the engine.

She peeked through the back window and saw Blake sprawled out and moaning. From the god-awful smell that hit her when she opened the door, it was clear that someone had been puking.

With as much gentleness as she could muster, she lifted Blake's shoulders, slipped into the seat, and laid his head on her lap. His forehead was warm to touch and his breath reeked of alcohol.

Sam glanced back as he drove and offered an apologetic smile.

"Should I remove his beanie? He's burning up."

Sam shook his head vehemently. "No, he wouldn't like that. He's just had too much to drink. Don't worry about him."

Before she could answer, Blake took her hand from his forehead. "Hey . . ." He drawled the one word into four syllables in full drunken form.

"Hey, you," she whispered.

Blake gave an innocent smile. His good eye was closed, and in the glow of the little light from the dashboard, he almost looked peaceful. Relaxed.

Forgetting about her own fears became easy as he held her hand for the duration of the short drive back to his place. Even in his inebriated state, he brought her comfort. She felt safe.

Sam eased Blake's Jeep in the driveway and turned off the engine. "Here, let me help you inside first, and then I'll come get him."

She was going to refuse but Blake nudged her, slurring out his order. "*Go.*"

"Going." Sam grinned, walked around the car, slipped an arm around her waist, and hefted her out of the car.

"This isn't necessary. I can walk." Jennifer tried to push off his chest.

"My pal might be out of his mind, but he made it clear that I get you home, safe." Sam stopped at the front door while he retrieved the keys. "And by the looks of it, your foot isn't doing great."

"How can you tell?" she asked.

They headed toward Blake's bedroom.

"I happen to be familiar with the scent of blood," Sam said, lowering her on the edge of the bed.

"I should stay in the spare room. He should take his bed—closer to the bathroom."

Sam raised an eyebrow. "Knowing that man, he would beat the crap out of me if I put you in the other room. I distinctly remember him mentioning that he had you sleeping in here before you left."

Jennifer had no idea why she blushed. Trying to cover her discomfort with the arrangement, she made a stupid decision. "Then put him here, too. That way I can take him to the bathroom if he needs to go."

Yeah, that explains everything.

Sam nodded and left the room only to return moments later with Blake hanging over his shoulder like a sack of potatoes. "Where do you want him?"

There was a hint of humor in the question, but she ignored it. "Here." She pointed to the right side of the bed, where the clock was more visible to Blake.

Sam eased Blake onto the bed and proceeded to remove Blake's shoes. "Whatever you do, don't remove his patch, and leave the beanie alone." Sam's warning was clear.

She took advantage of the resource available to find out more about this enigmatic man passed out beside her. "Why?"

"He doesn't take kindly to pity, sympathy, or whatever it is that most ladies throw his way." Sam's gaze traveled down to her injured foot. "I should look at that before I go."

"It's okay. I can do it." Her foot throbbed as though it had a life of its own and made it known that her decision to leave had been childish and stupid.

"I'm afraid I can't leave until I check it out. Blake has been so worried about you."

Jennifer peered at Blake's sleeping form. "He's been worried?"

"Yep. So let me look at it," Sam said.

I made him worry?

She blushed, looking away quickly, but nodded, and Sam went to the bathroom. She heard the drawers being opened and he came back with a first aid kit.

Sam pushed a chair at the edge of the bed and laid a clean towel on top. "Prop your foot on this. Tell me if it hurts, okay?" Sam began removing the bandage and she heard him sigh. "Thank your lucky stars it isn't as bad as I thought. You just seem to be a bleeder."

Jennifer hissed when Sam applied the antiseptic. In order to get her mind off the burning pain, she focused on the nagging question in her head. "Why was he drinking?"

If Sam wanted to tell her to mind her own business, he didn't let on. He looked at her and shrugged. When he finished wrapping her foot with a fresh bandage, he inspected his handiwork and grinned. "You should be okay. Just stay off the foot."

"Thank you so much."

Sam moved across the room and sat on the swivel chair. Just as she started to get uneasy with the silence, he spoke. "I've been inviting him for drinks. You know, to get out of the house and to enjoy life a bit. He loves music, but since the blast, he hasn't done anything. He hasn't picked up his guitar. Nothing. Then, this afternoon, I was surprised but took it as a positive sign when he didn't argue with my invitation . . ." He swirled the chair around like a child trying to stall.

"And?"

"I dropped by to pick him up so we could drive together. He seemed distracted, angry even, but with Blake, there's no asking him unless you want your head bitten off and served à la carte, so I left it alone. We dropped by your house before we headed to the bar, and still he didn't say anything. After several drinks, he started unloading. Maybe it was his anxiety that got the best of him, but then out of the blue, he went up to the stage and started playing. He's good." Sam shook his head.

Jennifer didn't know what to say. She vaguely remembered Trent mentioning their group singing while Blake played the guitar occasionally during down time.

"If you don't mind me asking, why did you leave?" Sam watched her with intense green eyes that made it difficult to ignore him and his question.

"I left this afternoon and walked home."

"I didn't ask *when*. I figured that part out the moment I saw your foot."

"Blake's your friend. You know what he's like . . . how stubborn and rude he can be."

"I met Blake after his injury so I have no idea what he was like before the blast. One thing I can tell you, though, soldiers coming back from the war aren't just nursing physical injuries. They are also trying to deal with the emotional issues from what they've witnessed. As much as society proclaims support for returning vets, they aren't sure how to handle the psychological scars."

She felt silly for walking out and not facing the storm that was Blake. "I understand," Jennifer said, and she did. "I want to help him if he'll let me, but he's built these walls . . . I'm not sure he'll let anyone in. He's all over the place. For someone who claims he wanted to keep me safe, his behavior is contradictory."

Sam nodded. "Well, it takes time. He has to come to terms with his losses before he can accept the life that he has now. Blake is a great guy underneath that abrasive exterior."

Jennifer glanced at Blake's face. The harsh lines around his mouth were absent, and he resembled the man she'd met so long ago.

"He talked about you the whole time we were at the bar. 'Jennifer is brave. Such a pity Trent died. I wish I could find a woman like her. I won't forgive myself for treating her the way I did.' " Sam chuckled. "He's like a freakin' tornado when he's had enough to drink. And he wouldn't listen when I told him to stop." Sam shrugged and smiled a little. "That's when you called, and I kinda did the math."

"Are you telling me that he got drunk because I—"

Sam suddenly stood and glanced at Blake. "Well, if you think you can handle Romeo here, I'll lock up and go." He saluted and walked out, and then she heard the soft click of the front door closing.

Jennifer looked at Blake, and her heart ached. She was torn between wanting to touch him and hoping she had the strength to fight her growing attraction to this infuriating man. He was in a rut and she wasn't sure how to help him.

Blake stirred and then gurgled. His skin was almost a gray pallor.

Unsure exactly what he needed, she hopped to the bathroom and retrieved the wastebasket and placed it next to the bed.

As though he'd known what she'd done, he lurched to his side and retched.

Still not certain she was helping, she began rubbing his back in soothing circles and hoped for the best.

He flopped back on the mattress, his good eye fluttering and focusing on her. "I'm jus' glad you're home, Jenny."

In normal circumstances, the sight of a drunk-stupid man wouldn't have alarmed her, but this was Blake.

With all his medical concerns . . .

It was obvious Blake was hurting, and he needed someone with him.

Jennifer moved toward the foot of the bed and started tugging off his socks.

Just when she thought he had fallen asleep, Blake sighed and spoke in that way that was both irritating and comforting at the same time. "I shu'd be takin' care you, not t'other way around, ya know."

He's drunk. Just let him talk it out.

His breathing evened out, and she felt his cheek. Her palm burned on contact.

Not good.

Half running, half hopping, she hobbled to the bathroom, grabbed a washcloth, and soaked it with lukewarm water. She returned to find him removing the eye patch and rushed to put a finger on the cover to stop him. "Don't, Blake," she whispered.

His eye opened. "You're . . . skert." Blake gave a sardonic laugh.

She wasn't even sure if he knew what he was about to do. Jennifer decided to give a truthful answer even if Blake wouldn't remember what she said in the morning. It was more for her benefit.

"Never. I want to see you when you're ready." She dabbed his cheek with the washrag and worked in slow, soothing strokes on cooling his forehead and neck. "Why don't you try to get some rest? You had a lot to drink."

"No, no, no." Blake waggled his finger at her. "You . . . like that woman, you know, gonna leave, becuz I'm scary."

The woman Blake was comparing her to seemed to agitate him. He sounded like a man harboring deep emotional wounds.

Her chest constricted. "I'll be around if you want me," she said.

"Sleepies . . ." He jabbed the pillow several times. "Stay."

"Okay," she murmured, stroking his cheek to calm him down.

For what it was worth, her words seemed to comfort Blake as he relaxed and buried his head.

Once she was sure he was asleep, she snuggled against him. She gasped and sat straight up when she heard him speak.

"Trent, 'm takin' care of our girl."

Clear as a bell, he spoke of a promise she had been certain he'd forgotten. Her pride kicked into high gear as she considered being a part of this infuriatingly aggravating man's life out of some sense of obligation.

She sighed and leaned against the headboard to contemplate her options.

Jennifer woke up sometime in the middle of the night when she felt the bed dip. She glanced at the clock.

Ugh, two hours.

Blake was attempting to get out of bed.

She jumped up when she saw him wobbling. "Where are you going?" she asked, circling an arm around his waist to steady him.

He didn't even look at her. "I'm gonna sho'r."

Drunk showering . . . how fun.

"Can't you wait until morning?" she asked.

Blake heaved and cupped his mouth.

They awkwardly made their way into the bathroom where she guided Blake to the sink.

She turned around to give him a bit of privacy, but nothing came out.

"Sho'r," Blake said, and swayed toward the bathtub.

"I don't even think you can stand on your own. How do you figure you're going to stay upright the whole time?"

He grinned and wiggled his eyebrows. "You gonna hol' me?"

Excuse me?

It didn't sound as if he recognized her at all.

Deciding that reinjuring her foot was enough stupidity for one day, she said, "Sit here while I warm the water." She pulled the toilet lid down and patted the seat. Turning the shower knob, she waited until the water reached the desired temperature.

How do I get myself into these things?

"Can you stand up?" she asked.

Blake nodded and fumbled for the light switch, engulfing the small room in darkness. "You gonna creep out."

As he attempted to remove his clothing, Jennifer knew that she had to help. He could barely stand in his drunken state. There was no way he was going to get undressed without someone getting hurt.

"Hold on to me."

Blake hesitated then placed his palms on her shoulders for support.

When she pulled his pants down, she felt a jerk in his midsection. Not wanting to embarrass him by reacting, she tried not to falter as she removed his boxers.

"S'not what I . . . 'cause I'm not gonna—" Blake cupped his mouth once again. "I don't go round paying, you know, chicks for money. I mean sex. Or whatever. You know?"

In the darkness, there wasn't much she could see, but it didn't mean that her other senses weren't twice as sharp. She heard his uneven breathing, smelled the alcohol with each exhale, and felt the tautness of his body brushing against hers.

Once his shirt was removed, Blake groped for the shower.

Jennifer took his hand and led him inside without a word. The water soaked the sleeve of her shirt.

"Yoush'd join me." Blake tugged at her hand.

Jennifer closed her eyes and tried to slow her pounding heart with slow, deep breaths as her mind raced. Every sensible part of her screamed for her to march out of the bathroom, but there was a part of her that wanted to be with this man.

Big mistake. Big, big, huge mistake!

She opened her eyes and as they adjusted to the darkened room once more, she saw Blake standing under the warm spray, and she fought the urge to wrap her arms around him.

Yeah, yeah, whatever. You can deal with it later.

Trying not to appear too eager, she removed her wet clothes down to her underwear and tossed them on the side of the tub. "Go ahead and shower while I hold you."

Blake's proximity was already wreaking havoc, and she hadn't even touched him yet. She tried to maintain her distance as she placed her trembling hand against his back for support while trying to keep her foot from getting wet.

She watched Blake plant both palms on the tiled wall while water trickled down his muscular body. She had no idea when or how it had happened, but she realized she felt more alive when she was with Blake. And she wanted him, to be *with* him.

Holy hell, I'm falling for him!

It was clear that the man she had known all along was buried in the façade he'd built around himself.

As the soothing water cascaded down her body, Jennifer began to relax. The steam swirling around them added a subliminal eroticism she could no longer deny.

Blake turned around all of a sudden. "Gonna soap ya."

She wanted to ignore his effect on her, to refute her feelings for him, but it was turning out to be an impossible task. Blake began lathering her body, starting with her chest.

She closed her eyes and took pleasure in the feeling of his hands on her skin. If he had intended to avoid her sensitive areas, he wasn't succeeding. His rough hands brushed the tip of her nipple, making her shiver. Feeling alive for the first time in a long time, her eyes fluttered open and reality began to seep in.

"I—I think you're good to do this on your own." She tried to move away from him.

Blake held her arm, refusing to let her get away, drawing her closer to him as the warm water continued its invigorating caress on her skin. "You no like it?"

She watched his muscles ripple with every movement. Just when she thought that she was satisfied with being alone, Blake had come along. It had been so long since she had last felt lust, to want someone. His touch had the desired effect and it took a tremendous amount of restraint not to touch him back.

Jennifer gasped when his erection rubbed against her thigh.

Blake dropped the soap and tilted her chin up to him. " 'M gonna kiss you now." He swayed and braced his hand on the wall to steady himself.

Instead of taking the sane route and running away, Jennifer closed her eyes and waited.

Blake's lips descended on hers for a rough kiss.

Her response was fervent despite the nagging thought that he wouldn't remember any of this the next day. Jennifer arched her back, letting her breasts rest against his wet skin. He pressed closer, and all she could think of was his shaft rubbing the region where she wanted to feel him the most. She had the audacity to imagine Blake kissing the insides of her thighs, licking her before finding her sex.

He squeezed her butt cheeks. "Touch me," he whispered against her mouth.

She shook her head, not breaking their kiss, but her hand seemed to have a mind of its own as it slipped down to grip his erection. To make matters worse, her body undulated, and her legs spread apart as if it was the most natural thing to do.

Blake broke away from their kiss and grunted.

The sound made her blood pump, waking her desire even more. With deliberate motion, she let her palm glide back and forth, and he groaned.

Blake lifted her by the waist and pressed his forehead to hers.

She hitched and locked her legs around his hips.

"Takin' the woman now."

The right thing to do was to say no, to announce that it wasn't the right time, but she couldn't push him away. She didn't want to.

"Take me here, right now." Jennifer's response startled her, but her need for him went beyond the need to possess his body. It went deeper.

She grabbed a handful of his hair, and they kissed with unmistakable hunger and devoid of patience.

Blake responded by bracing her back on the tiled wall and lowered her entrance to his erection.

They groaned in unison as he filled her.

He shifted into a more comfortable position and let her slide down to his thighs.

In her lust-filled logic, she remembered his injury. "Blake . . . your legs."

"Hush." He increased the pressure.

Jennifer's moan rose to a crescendo as Blake pumped harder.

He suckled her breasts.

Nothing made sense, and she didn't care. All she could think about was the delicious friction of his shaft rubbing against her skin and her walls constricting into a tight knot around him. She was hot and perilously close to the edge.

Blake made grunting sounds while guiding her body in a rhythmic, pounding motion, and a moment later, he seized her mouth and jerked his release. He thrust even harder when her orgasm exploded and kept pumping until she could barely breathe in ecstatic bliss.

After usurping their last energies in savoring the magical connection, Blake rested his head at the hollow of her neck, his taut body relaxing. "Hot damn," he mumbled.

You can say that again.

Jennifer didn't trust herself to say anything.

Their bodies remained clasped for some time before he hoisted her back onto her feet.

After she wrapped her still trembling body with a towel, Jennifer helped Blake out of the shower and into clean clothes before leading him to bed.

She got dressed and climbed in next to him, too exhausted to think. A wave of guilt was beginning to gnaw at her by the time she fell into a troubled sleep.

Blake twitched awake from an unsettling sleep sometime in the early morning, unsure of what had happened after he'd had enough vodka to keep him floored for a lifetime. He blinked and tried to gather his bearings. Feeling bile swirling, he swallowed hard and tried to recall the events from the night before. He distinctly remembered refusing to answer Sam's questions, at least until he'd started drinking.

His buddy might as well think that he'd lost a grip on reality. He, the indifferent man who had stopped caring, often hid inside his cave, kept everyone at arm's length, and worried about nothing, had blurted his concerns about Jennifer like a blabbering idiot.

He sighed and turned to check on the time, but his arm was trapped under something . . . or someone.

He moved his free hand down, hoping. Relief washed over him when he found himself clothed.

He heard a decidedly feminine sigh from the pillow beside him and froze.

In his inebriated stupor, he must've picked up a woman and taken her home. He wasn't one who'd go for paid sex but his needs had likely taken over. If he had done the unthinkable, and the satisfied feeling in his gut told him he had, he prayed the woman next to him would leave as soon as she woke up. His fragile ego couldn't handle the pity-filled look he was sure would be on her face after seeing him without his layers of clothing.

Blake inched to the side to get a good look at the sleeping soul next to him. The pale early morning light lit the room just enough to make out the tiny form on her back and facing the wall. He trailed his hand down the woman's body to find her wearing a tank top and bikini. He traced a finger on her arm, loving her soft and smooth skin. Curiosity got the best of him and he reached for her chin and turned her to face him. Blake squinted and made out the contour of the woman's face. After so many years staring at her picture and watching from a distance, he had every line memorized, and his spirit deflated.

Fuck! What have I done?

Bits and pieces of the night before began to surface—the shower, her glorious body, and the inevitable outcome.

He closed his eye and tried to quell the panic building at a rapid speed. Self-loathing was a dangerous thing, and he was on the verge of drowning in it.

He ran his fingers over the fine strands of her hair. The beautiful honey-colored tresses that he had longed to touch were right at his fingertips. He imagined her kind, hazel eyes that offered more than compassion, but a refuge and a chance to forget his misgivings.

Blake wished that Jennifer was with him for a different reason, but they were victims of circumstance and the memory of a man they both loved. If he had forced himself on her, he would never forgive himself.

Instead of pushing her away like he knew he should out of sheer self-preservation, he cradled her closer to his heart.

Love, lust, unimaginable want, all topped off with alcohol, and the effect had proven disastrous. And as if the guilt wasn't enough, a nasty wave of paranoia hit him as he realized this meant Jennifer had seen his misshapen body. He might have gotten his way with her by feigning weakness and appealing to her kindhearted nature, but this was wrong.

What else can it be?

You can admit to yourself that you're falling for her and this was the only chance you can have her.

No, damn it!

A glutton for punishment, he pressed his mouth to her glorious mane, and inhaled. Her sweet vanilla scent seduced him.

I'll take whatever I can get.

He was determined to hold on to this false sense of security for the duration of the night because, in the morning, it had to be business as usual between them. He'd set it straight with Jennifer and apologize.

Jennifer burrowed deeper against him and her leg tangled with his.

Why did Trent have to die?

He'd had so much to offer Jennifer. A life of love, a home filled with laughter, and a long time together ahead of them.

It should have been him in Afghanistan.

Me, not Trent.

Then, with vivid clarity, he recalled the day he thought his friend was going out of his mind.

November 18, 2001

"I can't marry Jennifer," Trent said one afternoon during patrol break.

Standing on the dusty roadside on the outskirts of Kabul, Blake stared at his friend. "What the hell are you talking about? The frigid wind's done damage to your brain, dude."

Trent avoided Blake's gaze and pretended to watch the children playing in the street. "I'm not kidding. I can't marry Jennifer. I won't."

"What's the deal, T?"

Trent inhaled and exhaled a long, drawn out sigh. "I can't father a child."

Blake must have zoned out while staring at Trent, because his friend was calling his name when he snapped back into the present. "Does she know?" he asked.

Trent dismissed his inquiry with a wave of his hand. "No . . . let's leave it at that."

"So you just decided you're not going to marry her?" His voice rose. "Like she means nothing?"

"I don't want to hurt her in the long run. She told me after I proposed that she wanted children. She'd be miserable." Trent glared at the abandoned building before them.

The rest of the squad continued their patrolling duties.

Blake followed the others, but he was far from letting Trent off the hook. "You can't leave her high and dry, man." He looked over his shoulder to find Trent trailing behind him.

Tears pooled in Trent's eyes. "If you don't want her left like that, why don't you marry her?"

Incredulous, he pressed his lips into a tight line. He gripped his M16 until his knuckles turned white. "You're a bastard, aren't you? You have a good woman waiting for you, and you're going all hissy because you can't make babies? You're so fuckin' full of yourself."

"The way I see it, you love her, too. So marry her and give her the one thing I can't," Trent shouted.

Shane and Robert turned to check on them.

Blake raised his hand and gestured for them keep moving. "I'm not in love with your girlfriend." The denial left a bitter taste in his mouth, but what else could he say under Trent's close scrutiny?

"The hell you aren't. I see the way you look at her pictures. The way you hang on to everything I say about her. Connor, you're much more transparent than you care to believe."

―∿∿―

That had been the last time they'd addressed the matter. Blake had avoided the topic like a plague. Sure, Trent had read him like an open book, but he hadn't let it happen again.

And that fateful day, his last words had been for him to take care of their girl. A man's dying wish. Whether Trent had lived or died, Blake had known that he was always going to watch over his friend and his wife because they were a big part of his life. Trent had been his best friend.

Sure . . . let yourself believe that's all there is, Connor.

Blake closed his eyes and let the sad memory drift away.

God, I miss him so much.

Life had never been the same after that.

He spent the remaining hours of the waning morning holding Jennifer and loving the warmth her body provided him. He could hold her like this for the rest of his life, but what woman would want damaged goods? And he was definitely broken. He wasn't going to make a fool of himself because he knew damn well that he was better off alone.

The sunlight was streaming through the window by the time he awoke again. His first inclination was to check on Jennifer, and he found her still fast asleep in his arms. He ran his fingers along her hair, loving the feel of the strands brushing his skin.

Jennifer stirred, and he froze, but instead of opening her eyes, she snuggled closer, a contented smile on her beautiful face.

He inched closer to the headboard and leaned against it as his body reacted to her nearness. He battled the desire.

God, I'm an animal.

The last thing he needed was a hard-on with Jennifer close enough to feel it. She deserved someone better, a man who would cherish her.

Why can't I remember the important stuff?

All he had were vague flashbacks with nothing concrete to base his next move on, and trying to force the memories back only left him flustered.

What if nothing happened?

Glancing at Jennifer, his gaze traveled down her long and pleasing legs, lingering on the one that had been tangled with his not so long ago, before moving to her bandaged foot with . . . crusted bloodstains. Just like that, his mood changed from night to day and he sat upright in bed.

"Jennifer, wake up!" He gave her shoulders a vigorous shake. And another.

"Huh?" Jennifer's eyes fluttered open, and he saw a trace of smile when she focused on his face. "What time is it?" She scrambled to get up, not seeming to mind finding him beside her. If this was an act, she was putting up a remarkable performance.

"You fuckin' left when you're supposed to be off that foot." He pointed at her leg. "Look at it."

Jennifer looked down and cringed. "I can't stay here if you keep yelling at me."

"If you keep insisting on breaking all records for stubbornness, then you deserve to get yelled at."

"If you weren't a total grouch, I wouldn't have left. You invited me to stay here, yet you bite my head off every single chance you get. You look at me like I'm a carrier of a disease. What is it, Blake? What do you want from me?" Her eyes blazed, practically daring him to deny her words.

He caught himself before the sharp retort sprang from his lips.

Jennifer was right. He hadn't been the perfect host. No matter how he felt about her, he'd insisted that she stay, and the least he could do was to be civil.

"I'm . . . sorry. I haven't been myself since . . ." He rammed his fingers through his hair and remembered what might have happened between them last night. He dropped his gaze and shook his head. "About last night . . . I'm so sorry. Did I—"

Jennifer looked at him as if she was gauging his mood before she answered. "We're both adults, so don't worry about last night. It was a mistake. I shouldn't ha—"

"You're right. Forget what happened last night. Let's start all over again. Stay here until it's safe to go back to your house. I promise I'll stay out of your hair."

"That's not what I'm asking you to do. Can't we at least have a normal conversation where we don't skirt around each other like chickens with our heads cut off?"

Oh, Lord. This is going to be painful.

If it meant keeping her safe, he would grin and bear it. "I'll try . . . if you let me take care of that foot."

Jennifer's expression turned, and he wasn't sure if it was because she was hurting or upset with him.

"Sam already took care of it. He says I'm just a bleeder. There's nothing to worry about as long as I stay off it. I was going to change the bandage after we—" She looked away. "You needed help an—"

He felt his cheeks burn in mortification. "We what?"

God, how far would you go to spare my feelings?

He closed his eyes and chose his words carefully. "Did I say or do anything . . . offensive?"

She hesitated then shook her head. "You wanted me to stay . . . never mind, it's not important."

He sensed her reluctance, sure she was hiding something, but he decided it was best not to press for details that could hurt them both.

"Sit up and let me check the stitches." He pushed his body off the bed but the sudden activity made the room spin. "Damn!" He sat back down and gripped his head between his palms.

"What's wrong?" Jennifer scooted closer, and her legs brushed his bare skin.

He recoiled as though a bolt of lightning had hit him.

Any more of her vanilla-sweetened touches and he knew he wouldn't be able to keep his hands off this woman.

"A goddamn hangover." He closed his eyes and tried to gather his wits. She was swinging her legs off the bed when he caught her wrist. "Where the hell are you going?"

"I'm going to get you a glass of water and an aspirin." She tried to shake out of his grasp.

"Didn't I tell you to stay off that foot? Don't you ever listen?" He immediately regretted shouting. "Damn it, Jennifer. Will you please let me take care of you and stop mothering me?"

The look on her face said that she'd had enough of his childish tantrums and his ever-changing mood. She gritted her teeth before giving him a good lashing. "Is that what you think I'm doing, Blake?"

He didn't answer.

"You're so wrapped up in your pity party that you're driving everyone away. I wanted to be your friend, but it seems like you're incapable of letting anyone in because you're afraid."

He started to open his mouth but clamped it shut.

"I know you think I pity you, but I don't. You have enough for all of us. Sure, half of your face is burned and you lost an eye, but life doesn't stop there. You still have a lot to offer. You turn your mother away because she loves you and she wants to care for you. It is obvious that a woman hurt you in the process, and you think the rest of us are out to get you. Wake up and smell the coffee, Blake. Life continued whether you like it or not, and you have to catch up."

Jennifer pried his fingers off her wrist and hurried out of the room.

The minute she cleared Blake's bedroom, Jennifer felt stupid for her childish outburst and careless for walking on the foot that was still screaming. Despite the doctor's warning to stay off it, her foot had been subjected to relentless punishment for the past two days.

Jennifer gasped at the sharp, stabbing pain that snaked up her leg. She braced her palms on the wall and pressed her lips together to keep from crying out.

Drew bounded toward her, wagging his tail with eagerness.

"Stay, Drew," Blake commanded, and was by her side in an instant, wearing a worried expression. "What's wrong?" Without waiting for an answer, he wove his arm around her waist, lifted her, and walked her to the living room sofa.

Blake's arm rubbed her breasts as he deposited her on the couch. The instant thrill she felt caused her to shrink back, embarrassed by her body's immediate reaction to his touch.

Something flashed across Blake's face at her reaction, but he said nothing as he held her gaze instead.

What in the world do I do now?

For a moment, all she wanted was a kiss. It was awful, but she couldn't ignore the burning thrill within her. It was wrong for her to expect more from their temporary arrangement. There was nothing between them, and the sooner she got that through her thick skull, the better off she would be.

She tried to create a little distance between them, but Blake wouldn't let go of her waist. He refused to break eye contact, and flustered, Jennifer inched her face away, scared at the possibility that he might see right through her and guess how she felt.

I don't want to feel anything. I can't.

Her gaze dropped to his mouth, a mere inch away, then back to his eyes.

Blake didn't move. He kept watching her, making her more uncomfortable with each passing second.

Do something. Say something.

"I—"

"I won't apologize for doing this," he said.

And just like that, he captured her mouth for a long kiss—so gentle and so different from the previous night. Her mind reeled at the delicious fusion and each twining of their tongues.

Jennifer closed her eyes and surrendered to the pleasure he offered. She prayed this moment would never end. This man, though infuriating, had the power to send her mind into a tumultuous spin. Giving in to her yearning, she let her hands glide across his shoulder to pull him closer, and clasped them behind his neck.

Without breaking their kiss, Blake settled on top of her while bracing one hand on the sofa.

The feel of his strong, hard chest rubbing against her breasts made her freeze for a moment.

If he asked for her to give in, she'd be powerless to say no. She wanted this, and him. After what seemed like a blissful eternity, he abruptly ended their kiss.

An expression of guilt etched his rugged face. "Stay there and don't move." His voice was thick with emotion. "I will check on your foot when I get back."

Lips still puckered and tingling, all she could do was to stare at him.

Blake disappeared into the hallway and came back with a pillow, the first aid kit, and Drew on his heels.

Jennifer noticed the slight limp he was trying to conceal, but she kept her mouth shut, not wanting to ruin the good vibe between them.

He placed the kit on the coffee table and brought the pillow to her head.

"Hoist yourself up," he said. For once his tone lacked the sting he often used when ordering her around. Then Blake proceeded to gather two more throw pillows and lifted her legs, propping them on the cushion. "Comfortable?"

She nodded, not trusting herself to speak.

He began unwrapping the bloodstained cloth and frowned. "You have to stay off this foot until it heals. It's only getting worse." She tried to sit up but he stopped her. "Let me take care of it."

Obedience didn't come easy for her. Being on her own for so long had made her too independent and proud, but the abrupt change in Blake's behavior had made her compliant, in part because she was curious just how long it would take before he reverted back to his old grouchy self.

Blake tended to her foot with deft hands and light touches. Genuine concern flashed across his face each time she flinched. In the blink of an eye, the old Blake emerged—the caring man beneath the gruff exterior that she recognized from her memories.

"You seem like you know what you're doing."

Blake looked up with amusement twinkling in his lone eye. "We had to learn basic first aid. We didn't always have a medic close by, and we had to be able to fend for ourselves until real help arrived." He tilted his head and inspected his handiwork.

"What?"

"Well, a couple of sutures reopened. Nothing to worry about. I'm afraid they can't be stitched back, so I had to apply some butterfly stitches. If you keep off the foot for several days, it should heal just fine." He grinned, seeming pleased with himself, and flipped the kit's lid closed.

She liked Blake this way. Relaxed, and without the ever present harsh lines around his mouth.

"I can't have you waiting on me hand and foot. I have to pull my weight around here if you want me to stay."

Blake regarded her for a moment, and she returned his gaze with nonchalance despite her heart hammering against her chest. In this rare moment of casual and friendly atmosphere, she wished time would stand still.

"Here's the deal. If you stay off that foot for forty-eight hours, I will get off your back and be as pleasant as an angel." He smiled and extended his hand, and her heart almost melted.

Oh, no you don't. You're not charming your way with me.

She remembered how he used to be—self-assured, charismatic, and attractive to anything in a skirt. He still was, in fact, and she could vouch for it. He was too handsome, virile, and potent for his own good.

Too potent.

Someone she must avoid at all cost if she meant to protect herself from impending heartache. As soon as she was on her feet and her window was fixed.

Despite her unwillingness to be sucked in by his charm, she reached out to clasp his warm hand. "Deal. No snapping, no biting my head off, and no ordering me around."

"Fine. But . . . if you do *anything* stupid, I can't promise to behave." He grinned.

Jennifer knew that agreeing had disaster written all over it, yet she had given her word, and forty-eight hours wasn't that far away.

She held his gaze and opted to change the subject. "I'm starving."

"Just stay here, and I'll rustle us some eggs and bacon." He walked over to the entertainment center to retrieve the remote control.

"Do you have anything healthy?"

He stopped flipping the channels and gawked at her as if she had sprouted horns. "I thought bacon and eggs were healthy?"

He laughed and she joined in while Drew barked with excitement.

"I think you may have missed the memo. It loses the healthy tag if you eat it every day. Just think of the grease wrapping your arteries."

Blake wrinkled his nose and continued flipping the channels. "And what alternatives do you propose?"

"How about cereals rich in fiber? Not like a body can't use the help, you know." She winked, feeling bold enough to crack a joke.

"No, thank you. I'm as regular as . . . never mind. I don't have anything healthy at the moment, but we can go grocery shopping later and you can pick the stuff you want."

This was the side of Blake she had almost forgotten.

I won't survive the day if he turns that charm on full blast.

"Jennifer, is everything all right?"

She blinked. "Why?"

He sat on the foot of the couch and ran a gentle finger over her bandaged foot. "You're looking pale."

It took her a moment to realize that she had been staring. She swallowed before saying the first thing that came to mind. "You said I have to stay off my foot."

He placed the remote on the table, settling on some game show for background noise. "Who says you're walking? I'm going to carry you to the Jeep. We'll go to the drive-through grocery, and you can shop from there."

Apart from the idea of him carrying her and risking the effects of his closeness again, a trip to the grocery sounded harmless enough.

"What if I use my crutches?" she asked, closing her eyes in anticipation of another outburst.

Blake laughed, an honest to goodness belly laugh that echoed around the room. "Superman is at your service. Don't waste the opportunity." He flexed both biceps. He didn't give her a chance to respond as he whistled and left for the kitchen with Drew following him.

She heard the sliding door open and the sound of the dog's paws padding into the backyard, and then Blake chuckled.

This man is giving me whiplash!

—◦◦◦—

Blake hummed a tune the entire time it took for him to prepare their breakfast. He even found a moment to play with Drew while the bacon sizzled in the skillet. He had to check himself several times to keep from grinning and making a fool of himself in front of Jennifer.

Jennifer must think he was an idiot, but he didn't care. She had agreed to stay with him, and stay off her foot. Even if he knew last night's drinking debacle could not happen again, it was a price he was willing to pay. He still had no idea how she ended up in his bed and in his arms, but all he needed were better details from Sam. There wasn't a doubt in his mind that he'd never hear the end of the man's teasing. Regardless, he was happy that she was safe with him.

Is she?

"Drew!" Blake summoned and Drew raced back into the kitchen. "Good boy." He patted the dog's head and directed him to his water dish. "I bet you're thirsty after that long exercise." After washing his hands, he poured their coffee and filled their plates with food.

"Jennifer?"

She didn't answer.

He stepped around the corner and saw the steady rise and fall of her chest and realized that she must've dozed off while he was preparing breakfast.

Her arm rested on her forehead, and he had to control the urge to tangle through her glorious hair that was splayed out like a fan of feathers.

This woman was a ball of kindness, spunk, beauty, and perfection rolled into one. It was no wonder Trent had been head over heels in love with her. It didn't hurt that she had a mouth on her, too. She was one of the few people he knew who spoke their mind without the need to apologize for being frank.

Blake continued to watch her, debating whether or not to rouse her. After several minutes, he leaned forward and gave her shoulder a gentle shake. "Hey, breakfast is ready."

It took several more nudges before she surfaced from a rather deep sleep. The hand that had rested on her forehead brushed his arm, and electric currents jolted him in spite of the cotton sleeves covering his arms.

Get a grip, Connor.

"Mmm . . . that smells so good." Her eyes fluttered open. Those bright hazel eyes that could light up the room looked lazily up at him.

Concealing the tenderness that washed through him, he tried to appear distracted by the task of picking her up. He didn't trust himself to say a word while they ate in silence.

For a change, the lack of conversation was not due to tension. It was comfortable and neither one of them seemed compelled to say anything until they were already nursing their second cup.

Jennifer broke the silence. "Tell me, how long have you been staying in this house?" Her eyes widened almost immediately, and she looked as though she regretted asking the question. "I-I-I mean, I was surprised when Captain Norwalk gave me your address."

Blake felt his mood darkening and sensed Jennifer bracing for an onslaught of his anger. He took a deep breath, resigned to keep his end of their deal. "After I was discharged from the hospital, I came here so I could keep an eye on you, just like Trent wanted." He looked away. This bargain was going to cost him a lot more than he had anticipated.

"Why?" Her question sounded so innocent.

He swung his gaze back to her. "Because I'm a man of my word."

Jennifer's lips thinning didn't escape his notice. She raised the cup to her mouth and took a quick sip, set it down, and smiled. "You're a real good friend to Trent," she said, sounding wistful.

Admit it, already. It is more than that.

He wasn't ready to accept that Trent had been right all along. He wasn't ready to concede that his obsession for Jennifer was the reason his relationship with Katrina had been doomed all along. He had managed to prevent a meaningful relationship from blossoming. Instead, he'd repeatedly accused her of pitying him. That's why it hadn't come as a surprise when Katrina had left him for another man. It had been clear back then that she was better off without him, but placing the blame on her had been a way to take the focus away from his affection for another woman.

Jennifer's palm closed on his. "Hey, what's on your mind?" she asked.

He shook his head and forced a tight smile. "Another cup?"

"Are you going to have the energy to keep carrying me to the bathroom?"

He answered with an indulgent grin and refilled her cup.

The deep rumbling sound of a helicopter passing by on its way to Edwards Air Force Base roused Blake from his sleep.

He glanced at the clock and groaned.

Same shit, different day. Too damn early.

He'd been stuck in this schedule for what felt like forever. As usual, he'd beaten the alarm clock yet again.

Out of habit he reached for the eye patch and fitted it onto his face. Remembering that his appointment was coming soon, he felt a familiar sense of dread at the idea of another trip to the doctor's office. Though this one would be painless, the apprehension and discomfort of the upcoming consultation left him feeling sick to his stomach.

He recalled the unending trips to the hospital for skin grafts, debridement, and therapy. Those had been the ensuing hell that had followed the nightmare of Afghanistan. His distaste for anything doctor-related had led to an insistence that he could do without all of them and foregoing therapy far longer than he should have.

It had been irresponsible of him, but back then, he hadn't seen the point. He had already been in a tremendous amount of pain, and the additional exercises had left him physically tired and emotionally drained. If he wanted to punish himself even more, all he'd had to do was look at his pre-accident pictures. That was enough to send him shuddering.

By choice, he had been postponing the trip to the eye doctor for the same reason. He didn't understand the point of wearing a prosthetic eye to replace the unsalvageable one. With Sam and his parents' prodding, he had conceded and made an appointment.

During the phone consultation, the ocularist had given him assurances that the process was fast and painless. His first scheduled visit would consist of taking an impression of his eye socket, shaping a plastic shell and matching the color of the irises.

Painless, huh? Yeah, sure. Right.

He shoved the thoughts of the dreaded appointment aside in favor of getting breakfast ready before he had to leave for rehab. It would be a good time to extract information from Sam and shed some light on the parts he couldn't remember from two nights before. He hoped for Jennifer's sake that his drunkenness hadn't made her uncomfortable.

Drew whined, no doubt anxious to get their morning routine started.

"Hey, boy. Good morning to you, too."

The dog got up and gave a good shake, creating a considerable amount of noise as his nails scraped the bare floor.

"Keep it down, Drew. We don't want to wake the lady this early."

His four-legged friend seemed to understand and sat straight, ears perked up, and waited for his order.

Stretching, Blake extended his legs a fraction, just enough to release the rigidity of his limbs from the hours of inactivity. He repeated the stretches, not pushing too hard to avoid pain, and he got off the couch. He cracked his back twice, not sure sleeping on the couch was such a good idea. Then again, he wouldn't want Jennifer sleeping anywhere but his bed.

Man, that sounds good.

Shaking the wicked picture from his mind, he opened the door with care, hoping the wood wouldn't squeak this time.

Blake grinned when the door cooperated and he tiptoed to the bathroom across the hall. He finished his morning ritual without even glancing in the mirror. The last thing he needed was to feel the disgust. Besides, he didn't recognize the man staring back at him. Though most of his hair had been spared from the cookout, the side of his face had retained the scarring typical of burn victims—shiny, with uneven skin. Every single day he vacillated between two sentiments—glad to be alive and asking why he hadn't died that day.

If he couldn't bear to look at himself, how could he expect others to endure the torture?

Before he allowed that train of thought to sink his mood any further, he finished dressing. It took him several tries before he could snap the vest in place, due to the limited rotation of his shoulders. It came and went, and according to Sam, his missed appointments were bound to reflect the negative effects. True, the more therapy he attended, the better his body felt, but it didn't change the fact that the road to normalcy would be long and arduous.

Shaking the negative emotions that started to creep back in, he padded barefoot along the hallway with Drew in tow. He went straight to the cupboard and retrieved a box of high-fiber cereal, slipped it under his arm, and balanced two bowls, spoons, and a carton of milk.

Yeah, breakfast of champions.

It made him wonder if this healthy breakfast was enough to tide him over until lunch.

After he returned to the fridge and grabbed the carton of orange juice and fresh fruits, he went to his bedroom to check on Jennifer. He stood just outside the doorway, uncertain if he should wake her, when he heard running water coming from the bathroom.

He knocked, and when he heard a muffled answer, he pushed the door open. "Are you ready for breakfast?" he asked through the bathroom door.

A gurgle sounded before Jennifer answered, "Be out in a second."

He surveyed the area and found traces of her; a lip balm, a small spiral notebook, and a tattered picture. He walked closer to get a good look, feeling a bit guilty for invading her space, but he couldn't stop himself.

The photo was of him and Trent leaning on a concrete wall, garbed in their camos, and holding their rifles. It had been taken in their third year of service, as evident in their sullen expressions. He remembered Trent writing on the back of the photograph—melancholic and homesick.

Blake's chest tightened at the memory, and he was caught off guard when Jennifer spoke from behind.

"I carry it with me all the time," she said in a quiet voice.

He turned around. There were no words. They both missed Trent, and that was the extent of what he would allow himself to admit today. "Let's eat," he said.

If Jennifer had wanted to say something, she seemed to have changed her mind and pressed her lips together.

Without a word, he slipped an arm around her waist and swept her off her feet.

"All this lifting is not good for you," Jennifer said after he deposited her on the chair.

Blake took the chair opposite her and forced a weak smile. "It's the exercise I need."

They ate in silence but it was far from comfortable. He knew for a fact that Trent was very much in her mind. Even if he had something to offer her, his friend would always be the big, ever-present figure keeping him from giving himself to the woman he loved.

———

After Blake got her situated on the couch with everything he anticipated she might need, Jennifer stared at the television while her mind wandered to the whirlwind of events in the last thirty-six hours. Sure enough, thinking of Blake's kiss still made her head spin. His touch had left her heady, breathless, and more confused than ever. She couldn't make heads or tails of his actions and wasn't ready to recall what had happened in the shower. Some things were better left in the dark, where they belonged. If Blake had no recollection, or refused to broach the subject, then she had no intention of bringing it up.

What does he want from me?

He had mentioned that he was a man of his word. Did that mean when his babysitting days were over, he'd walk out of her life and disappear? Or did his promise to Trent go beyond the obvious? Contradicting actions aside, one thing was clear. He was physically attracted to her and the idea scared her to the point of wanting to flee.

"The guy has enough baggage to sink the Titanic," she muttered.

Was physical attraction enough for her? There was no denying her feelings for him went beyond raw appeal. The man had touched her heart in the simplest ways. The gentle way he held her, providing comfort and security. Only one man had ever made her feel as safe, but she hadn't felt the same pull as she did now.

This was definitely trouble waiting to happen. With everything he kept locked up inside him, she wasn't sure she had what it took to chip away at his walls. Trent, bless his heart, had told her all along that his best friend needed a sensitive woman who would love and understand him.

Had Trent foreshadowed—

The shrill ringing of the house phone jerked her off the Blake train of thought. She hopped on one foot to the kitchen, hoping the call would be good news from Officer Cortez.

"Hello?"

"This is the office of Doctor Dent. Is this Mrs. Connor?"

Mrs. Conno—

"Um, no. I'm—"

"I'm calling to confirm his appointment this time."

Her curiosity was piqued. "What kind of appointment?"

"He's been canceling on us, and Dr. Dent is a busy man. If he misses his eye consultation again, I'm afraid I won't be able to put him on the schedule until the end of this year."

Oh my.

"I'll make sure he doesn't miss this time."

I will?

"That would be a good idea."

"When is the appointment and what does he need to do?"

"All he has to is show up tomorrow at nine in the morning."

"He'll be there," Jennifer said, sounding so sure.

After hanging up the phone, she felt guilty for overstepping her boundaries. What made her so sure Blake would go? He was unpredictable and who knew how the man might react once he found out that she'd dipped her foot into his business again.

Rationalizing her dumb, but well-intentioned meddling, she hobbled back to the sofa and put her feet up. After all, she was just looking after his best interests.

She was figuring out the best way to tell Blake about the phone call when she realized the steady thumping was insistent knocking on the door. With clumsy movement, she hurried and hopped to the door to answer the caller.

Jennifer peeked through the peephole and saw a couple standing outside. She opened the door tentatively.

"Jennifer?" a gorgeous older woman with platinum blond hair and familiar sparkling blue eyes asked.

She smiled and opened the door wider. "Yes?"

"We're Blake's parents. I'm Claire and this is Jack. Is he home?"

The elderly man behind Claire dipped his head slightly. As tall as Blake with similar features, Jennifer saw who Blake took after.

"Hello, Mr. and Mrs. Connor. Blake's not home at the moment, but I'm sure he'll be back in a bit. Would you like to come in and wait?"

"Yes, thank you. Please, call me Claire." Blake's mother smiled and tugged at her husband's arm to follow.

Jennifer stepped back to give them enough room to enter. "I'm so sorry for the mess, but I've been camping here in the living room." She began to clear her things on the coffee table when Blake's mom stopped her.

"Child, go sit. I think that's the reason why Blake wants you here with him. So you can be off your feet and resting, right?"

Jennifer had been reminded of her mother the first time she'd spoken with this woman, but here, now, in full view of Claire's warm and cheerful personality, a lump formed in her throat.

Jennifer did what she was told. Blake's mother sat down on the recliner and turned to her husband.

"Dear, can you get the groceries from the car?"

Groceries?

"Are you sure that you should be cooking right away? You haven't even talked to Blake yet. We might be intruding," Jack said, eyeing Jennifer with a cautious smile.

"Oh, pooh. The boy needs to eat something more nutritious than takeout."

With a worried expression, Blake's dad went to fulfill his wife's request.

Jennifer looked up to see the older woman smiling at her.

"Why don't you tell me about yourself?"

Jennifer fidgeted.

What should I say?

"Um, I live not too far from here. I used to live in San Francisco with my aunt before she passed away. Then I relocated here after that."

"How do you like living in a hot place like this?" Blake's mother seemed sincere, but Jennifer had a sinking feeling that she also had aspirations of playing cupid.

"It has its charm. I like living away from the big city, for a change."

"I think you're right. I just never understood why Blake wanted to live here, away from us." Claire shook her head. "How did you meet him?"

Jennifer hesitated and looked down at her hands.

Truth or make something up?

She wrung her hands together and debated her answer.

This woman is Blake's mother, for God's sake. She'll catch any lie you try.

"Trent. Blake's friend and I were engaged to be married."

Mrs. Connor's eyes widened and her mouth dropped slightly open. After several silent seconds, she smiled. "Well, I'm glad to meet a friend of my son."

Their conversation was interrupted as Jack walked in with bags of groceries. "Where do you want this?"

Claire looked relieved for the distraction and patted Jennifer's knee. "Jennifer, stay put. If you need anything, just let me know. Let me help you, dear." She took one bag from her husband and proceeded to the kitchen.

Jennifer was left wondering about the older woman's hesitation but let it go, and for the next hour, she tried to concentrate on work and answering her neglected e-mails while the aroma of a home cooked meal drifted around the house.

—∿∿—

"Talk," Blake demanded as soon as he spotted Sam behind his desk.

The place was quiet and a perfect time to grill his friend for information about the events of a couple of nights ago.

Sam glanced up from the mound of paperwork on his desk, raised an eyebrow, and chuckled. "Where do you want me to start?"

Blake worked on removing his shirt and vest while he spoke. "From the beginning. How did Jennifer end up back at my house?"

Sam walked to the sink and lathered up. "You sound like you regret asking me to pick her up." He glanced over his shoulder at Blake.

Surprised, Blake tried to jog his memory, but couldn't recall making any such request. "I remember bits and pieces after I started drinking." He gritted his teeth while shifting his body to a comfortable position on the therapy table.

Sam went to work right away on his shoulders, massaging the tender skin and the tight muscles underneath. "Well . . . you drank like a fish to begin with. No matter what I said, you kept ordering one after the other, so I became the designated driver and a part-time psychologist."

"Keep talking."

"You went on stage and gave the crowd a little show."

"*What?*"

"Yep. Man, you're good. You should consider doing it for a living."

Stunned, he turned and stared at Sam. He knew he should have kept his big mouth shut about the music. "I have a job," he retorted.

Wha—a job. Really?

Sam snorted and moved on, working on rotating Blake's arm.

"Then what?"

"You were yapping about Jennifer leaving because you couldn't keep your temper in check. You kept repeating that she's your responsibility." Sam walked away only to return a few minutes later with a silicone gel and continued where he'd left off. "You were harping about looking for her everywhere, and how you wouldn't forgive yourself if anything happened to her."

He didn't have to be drunk to be certain that he'd never have forgiven himself for driving her away.

"So when she called and asked to be picked up, you crawled out of the bar to get to her." Sam chuckled. "We picked her up from her house, all scared and tearful, then she sat in the backseat with you. It is obvious that the woman cares about you, bro."

He turned and glared at his friend. "Nah." He chalked it up to pity and an honest-to-goodness instinct to mother. That was inherent to women, and he hated it.

"When we got to your place, she refused to let you sleep by yourself. She was concerned you might need help."

Again, Blake refused to believe that Jennifer felt more than just an innate sense to nurture.

"Then you kept repeating that she's beautiful and . . ."

When his buddy paused, Blake looked up. "And?"

"You said you're in love with her," Sam said.

Heaven help me.

Blake pinned his friend with a hostile glare.

Sam shrugged. "You wanted the truth. I'm giving it to you."

Blake wanted to dispute Sam's claim, but how could he? He couldn't remember, so he kept his mouth shut for the duration of the therapy.

He drove home in a quiet daze and tried to sort through the load of emotions that hit from every direction. Had he really proclaimed his feelings out loud?

Damn the alcohol and damn me for slipping.

As Blake approached his house, he noticed his parents' car parked outside. He parked, eased out, and took a deep breath before he opened the front door to let himself in. It would take a lot to keep his emotions hidden, but he'd damn well keep trying.

He plastered on a fake smile and was about to sing a greeting when he heard her on the phone.

"Oh, Matt, I miss you, too. I'm sorry I didn't return your call. Sure, you can come and visit me," Jennifer said, sounding happy.

Too damn happy.

He muttered an oath and marched straight to the spare room.

From the corner of her eye, Jennifer saw Blake streak by. She had been so caught up with the good news that she had missed his arrival. Matt's announcement meant her world was about to change, and she would soon be living her dream.

She bid Matt adieu and placed her cell phone on the coffee table, deliberating how to approach Blake. She had read a few articles about the pain and suffering of burn victims, and how therapy, no matter how helpful, could be physically taxing. Although Blake hadn't shown any indication that he'd been suffering, she wasn't fooled. He was trained to suffer in silence and to keep his emotions in check. She had gathered that much from Trent, and with Blake being a proud man, she surmised that this was all a brave front.

With the aid of the crutches, she moved gingerly across the hallway until she reached the guest room door, and knocked.

"Go away," he shouted above the blaring noise that was AC/DC.

Jennifer glared at the door and turned around to go the kitchen. "Your parents are here, in case you didn't know." She was prepping an excuse for Blake when she heard him walking down the hallway dragging his feet.

Jennifer heard Claire humming a tune as she got closer.

She looked up from the stove when she saw Jennifer. "Is he home?"

"Yes . . ."

Claire's smile broadened the moment Blake made an appearance. "I made your favorite."

"Hi, Mom." Blake walked past Jennifer and gave his mother a kiss on the cheek. "It smells wonderful. Where's Pops?"

"He's on the patio. I also brought some homemade carrot cake."

"Awesome."

Jennifer detected the forced enthusiasm. If Claire noticed her son's withdrawn behavior, she didn't show any indication.

Blake made his way to the patio and flopped on the lounger next to his father.

Jennifer turned her attention back to Claire. "Is there anything I can do to help?" she asked.

"Stay off your feet before Blake jumps on us both." Claire grinned and winked. "Sit and just keep me company."

For the next few minutes, Claire kept up a steady chatter about the charities she was involved in, while Jennifer attempted to keep up. She caught herself glancing at Blake every now and then. He seemed relaxed with his dad, and she could see him throwing back his head in laughter a few times.

Lunch was delicious and for the next hour, the four of them settled on topics about local politics and market trend. Safe topics. Blake seemed more relaxed with each passing minute and Jennifer found herself offering a few of her own insights.

After the dishes were cleared, she excused herself from the group to give them a chance to talk as a family in private.

She must've dozed off after the satisfying lunch because the house was quiet when she finally woke up. She hated that she'd missed saying goodbye to Blake's parents, but it had been an overwhelming day, to say the least.

She stretched before getting up, and found a note on the coffee table with her name on it. Inside, Claire had apologized for not saying goodbye and promised to call again. Smiling, Jennifer reached for her crutches and made her way down the hall to check on Blake.

She knocked on the door once. When there was no response, she knocked again. "Blake?"

"Go away."

"You said that earlier. What's wrong with you?" she asked, feeling her temper rise. She turned the knob and found him sprawled on the couch, his arm covering his face. Her annoyance was forgotten and replaced by worry. She hobbled closer and sat on the edge of the couch, dropping the crutches on the floor. "Blake, is everything okay?"

"Didn't you hear what I said?"

"Are you in pain? Can I do something?" She placed a hand on top of his and lifted it off his face. When their eyes met, she saw a mixture of pain and defiance in his.

"No, I'm fine. Just tired."

Bullshit.

Proud Blake wouldn't ever admit to such triviality, plus she saw something else from his expression. It was akin to resignation. Confused, she traced her fingers along the side of his cheek in a light caress.

"Tell me what's bothering you."

She expected rejection the moment she touched his face, but to her amazement, he didn't pull away. Instead, he leaned into her touch and closed his eyes.

"There are things that I have to accept. One of them is the situation I'm in," he said.

"What are you talking about?" she asked, not quite sure what his cryptic reply meant.

He pounded his fist on the couch. "Nothing. It's none of your business." He opened his eye and glowered at her.

She flinched, and just like that, the tender moment was gone. Her eyes burned and she turned her face away, blinking back the tears, not wanting him to see how his words had affected her.

Blake tugged at her hand, his tone softening. "Jennifer, c'mon. I didn't mean it. I'm just tired. The therapy zapped my energy and—"

"Will you tell me if something's wrong?" she asked, returning her gaze to him.

"Yes. I promise. Now tell me what you've been doing while I was away."

Jennifer sighed, not happy with the abrupt change of subject, but she wanted to share her piece of good news with him. "I got a call from my agent and a big name store wants to buy my designs."

Blake sat up, wrapped his arms around her, and pulled her head against his chest. "That is wonderful news!" He kissed her hair.

"In fact, he is coming tomorrow to bring the contract for my signature." Even without seeing his face, she felt his body stiffen and his heartbeat pound against her ear as if it might explode.

"Is that who you were talking to? That Matt guy you're missing?"

He sounded almost jealous, and the thought made her heart race. She decided to bait him and see where it led. "Actually, yes. Is there something wrong with inviting him over?"

Thick silence answered her. Just when she'd given up on getting any response out of him, he touched her chin and tilted her head up until they were looking into each other's eyes.

"I don't trust any man close to you."

Her heart fluttered. For the first time in her life, Jennifer felt love pouring out of her as it was meant to be. It had been so different with Trent. She had loved him, but not this way. Her gratitude and the comfort of their friendship had led her to accept his marriage proposal. With Blake, she operated on her body's response to his touches, on the overwhelming longing in her heart to be loved by him.

"Do you trust *you* to be close to me?" She turned her body until she was facing him and leaned forward to rest her forehead on his.

"Jennifer . . ."

Not allowing time to think, she captured his mouth for a kiss. She might regret it later, but it felt right and oh, so nice. The melding of their mouths was soft and tender, and she pressed her body closer.

Blake wound his arms around her waist and deepened their kiss. The warmth of his mouth excited her but the heat radiating from his body made her shudder.

Her bubble burst when Blake stiffened and pushed her away.

He stood, shaking his head. "This is wrong. I'm taking advantage of you. I can't do this. Not like this, and not with Trent in between us." Blake moved to the window and stared outside, his shoulders drawn tight beneath the light cotton, long-sleeve shirt.

"Trent's gone, and we will continue loving him, but I'm not sure what to make of this . . . thing between us."

"What do you think is going on between us, Jennifer?"

She flinched at his nonchalant tone, but he had a point.

What exactly is *going on?*

He hadn't really verbalized any feelings for her, but his actions betrayed all the times he tried to push her away.

She looked down at her hands knotted on her lap. "I don't know. It seems like you want me at times, but—"

"I haven't been with anybody for a while now. Having a desirable woman in my house is a difficult temptation to avoid."

His response and the memory of what had happened between them the other night made her feel cheap—a one night stand that he couldn't even discuss. He made it sound as though this was all physical between them.

Jennifer squared her shoulders and jutted her chin. "This is more than desire and temptation. This is deeper than that, and you know it. You're just stubborn and hiding behind Trent's shadow to avoid addressing it."

Blake's eye flickered then he gave a cold smile. "You can think anything you want. There's nothing between us. If you think a couple of little kisses are going to change me, you're mistaken. Trent is very much in this room, and everywhere I go. I see him every time I look at you, and I'd never allow myself to love you."

His words stung and the rejection rang in her ears.

Am I that bad?

"You're lying," she blurted. Emptiness ravaged within her despite her efforts to keep from letting his heartless proclamation rip her apart.

"I never lie about love, Jennifer."

He walked quietly out of the room, and before long, she heard the rumble of his Jeep as he pulled out of the driveway.

Left in tears, she grappled with disappointment and hurt. He had made it clear that she had been nothing more than a mere distraction, a body good for a minute of enjoyment. Despite the devastation she felt now, she would forever cherish the memory of their brief time together. She had bared her feelings to him, letting him see her vulnerability by admitting how she felt, and he had turned her away.

If Blake was only taking care of her because of some misplaced sense of honor then he could flush his intentions down the toilet. She was far too proud to take someone's pity and be a burden. She would stick to their deal, and then she'd be out of his life.

———〰———

"Back again? You look like shit," Sam said as Blake stepped through the doors again.

If I'd had any other place to go . . .

Being here made him feel too raw and too transparent because Sam always saw right through him.

"Shut it. I'm not in the mood." Blake flopped down in the chair.

Sam chuckled. "When are you ever?"

It was the truth. When had the clouds ever lifted? He was fast becoming his own worst enemy. He refused to give in to his feelings because he was scared of sharing the secret he'd kept for so long. That's why he'd doomed Katrina. She'd always known that his heart had belonged to someone else.

Sam pointed to the door on the far left. "Take the next room. It's vacant."

Blake shrugged.

At least Sam wasn't grilling him. He needed a place to hide and work through this. He'd made an ass of himself once more and insulted Jennifer in the process.

Not bothering to turn the lights on, he collapsed in the chair and closed his eyes.

November 20, 2000

Blake had been on a training mission with his unit in Africa, along with another group of Special Forces, when luck smiled on them in the form of clearance to return home until their next deployment. Great news, considering it meant they got the tail end of summer in the States, and the chance of Blake catching some good waves was still possible.

His first call should have been to his parents, but Blake had needs not even his staunchest supporters could satisfy.

Instead, fresh off the fifteen-hour flight from Sierra Leone, Blake waited for Katrina to answer.

The mounting stress relating to his job had been eating at him, and Trent's constant chatter about Jennifer was grating on his last nerve.

Sure, the woman was a perfect sight to behold, and one of those rare gems no one would want to part with, but Trent's nonstop worshipping had driven Blake to madness. The only way he knew to combat it was to find release.

"Hey, you're back?" Katrina sounded ecstatic.

Great start to my plans for the evening.

"Yeah. Are you free tonight?" he asked, not wasting time on pleasantries.

"Sure. My place or yours?"

"Your place at seven. I'll bring dinner and a bottle of wine."

As the sound of calming ocean waves accompanied them during their candlelit dinner, Blake felt a burst of energy and anticipated good things ahead. The braised lamb he'd ordered was cooked to perfection, and the cabernet complemented their meal and set the right mood.

Considering his motives, Blake liked to think that this showed he was still treating Katrina with respect.

"This is wonderful." Katrina took a sip from her glass and closed her eyes in contentment.

"It sure is," he answered, patting his belly. Nothing beat a great sit down dinner with an old friend.

"Another toast?" Katrina poised her glass in the air and waited for him to raise his. "Here's to you, for coming back home to me in one piece."

Blake cringed at the expressed sentiments, but put up a halfhearted smile. "Thanks." He clinked his glass to hers and downed the contents in silence. An image of Jennifer flashed through his mind, and he fought not to choke as the last swallow went down the wrong pipe.

Katrina walked over to him and hesitated. "Can I?" She gestured to his lap. When he cleared his throat and patted his thigh, she sat and wrapped her arms around his neck and rested her head on his shoulder. "I've missed you," she whispered.

Blake couldn't think of an answer over the primal hunger clouding his head.

The mood was perfect and the ambience couldn't have been any better with the beach only a few steps away. It was why he'd chosen her place over his. The sound of the ocean had always been his refuge with its calming effects.

"I have something for you." He fished inside his pocket, retrieved a little purple bag, and handed it to her.

"You got me a gift?" Katrina's blue eyes were wide, and Blake felt like an idiot.

Of course, the woman had expectations, and he was a big tease to dangle the possibility in her face.

She released his neck and sat down in the next chair. Excitement radiated from her as she loosened the cord on the velvet pouch, sneaking little glances in his direction.

"It's a necklace," he said, stopping any thoughts she might be entertaining of an engagement ring. He saw her disappointment quickly replaced by a forced smile.

"This is beautiful." She inspected the intricate details, running her fingers on the beads. "What is it made of?"

Blake leaned forward and took the jewelry from her.

Katrina lifted her hair to give him access.

"It is made of lappa beads made out of brass, recycled glass and clay. It's what they call Salone style. I thought you might like it." He clasped the lock.

Katrina turned and threw her arms around him, settling her mouth firmly on his.

"Thank you," she murmured after their lips parted. She straddled his hips when he coaxed her to sit on his lap.

Their lips reunited for another long and passionate kiss. Moments later, their heated desire found its way to the bedroom.

The night passed as they continued exploring the depths of their physical hunger. Driven by lust and a demanding need to forget the face and name that haunted him, Blake made love with Katrina over and over until sunrise peeked over the horizon. In spite of the satisfaction his body had enjoyed, his heart was empty and his life was far from perfect.

Blake woke up from his short nap feeling shittier than ever. Glancing around, he remembered swinging by the rehab center to hide. Sam had offered the room, and he must've dozed off.

Sam was finishing with another patient when Blake joined him in the common room.

Blake kept his distance until the teenager in a wheelchair was out of earshot. "Thanks for letting me crash here," he said in a quiet voice.

"Anytime, my man." Sam checked his watch and rubbed his belly. "Wanna grab a burger and a beer?"

Blake shook his head, remembering Jennifer alone in the house. "Not this time. I have some groveling to do." He headed to the exit, and Sam's chuckle followed him out the door.

He concocted a plan while making his way to his vehicle. His brusque behavior earlier called for damage control. He leaned on the door and dialed Jennifer's number, hoping she wasn't too upset to pick up.

The phone kept ringing. He was about to hang up when she answered.

"Hello?" Her voice sounded tentative.

Blake took a deep breath and hoped for the best. "I'll pick you up in thirty minutes. Dress comfortably." He made it sound like he wasn't expecting her to decline. Sometimes he wondered if it was even possible to revert to the old Blake, the man who had embraced what life had to offer because he had enough love to give.

When he heard a soft click, he knew his work was cut out for him.

He'd said hurtful things out of fear and a need to hide what he felt, but he wasn't going to let her snub deter him.

He eased the Jeep out of the almost deserted parking lot and turned left onto Avenue J. If begging for forgiveness was in order, a bouquet of flowers was a necessary tool to aid the effort. He turned into the flower shop's parking lot with every intention of finding the perfect arrangement.

"What can I get for you?" the woman behind the counter asked.

Blake hesitated, feeling out of his element. "I need a flower arrangement."

"Great. I can help you with that. Do you have anything in mind?"

When he shook his head, the lady led him to the cooler section and showed him several ready-made bouquets.

He studied each one but nothing caught his eye. "I want something much more special."

"What is the occasion?"

"I've been an ass." Blake rubbed his forehead, unable to believe that he just let a stranger in on his woes.

The woman laughed. "Okay . . . let's see. White flowers connote forgiveness."

"Uh-huh." He gave her a blank stare.

"Do you trust me to come up with something beautiful for you?"

Trust?

Beautiful?

Yep, that's Jennifer.

"Yes," he said.

While the lady started opening the refrigerated section and pulled flowers from buckets, he wandered around.

He felt a little silly, but it was too late now.

Women like flowers, right?

Or jewelry.

His teeth clenched as he recalled the mistake he'd made the last time he'd bought jewelry for a woman.

In less than twenty minutes, the florist called out and presented him with an array of elegant and fragrant flowers.

All Blake could do was grin.

Jennifer's gonna love them.

"What are the flowers?"

"Roses, oriental lilies, and some alstroemeria."

After he paid for the arrangement, he felt light on his feet as he banked on Jennifer's forgiveness being given without a hitch.

The rest of the drive home was spent in self-reflection.

When he reached his place, Drew began barking when he spotted him walking up the path.

So much for surprising Jennifer.

"Hey, boy, where's the beautiful lady?" he whispered, bending down to run his hand over Drew's shiny coat.

"She's right here."

Jennifer was seated on the sofa, looking glorious, and dressed in a floral sundress that showed more skin than he needed to see.

His gaze was immediately drawn to her low-cut neckline that revealed her rounded cleavage.

Damn it, Connor. Don't start.

Feeling the heat rising to his face, he looked up to catch Jennifer narrowing her eyes. It was another tongue-tied moment while Blake searched for something intelligible to say. Nothing came to him, and in an effort to avoid looking like an idiot, he took a step forward and offered the flowers to her.

Her face softened, and a little smile broke the ice. "Thank you." She sniffed the flowers. "They're lovely. What's the occasion?"

"It is step one of my attempt to beg for forgiveness." He hoped that his lighthearted tone would earn him another smile.

She smiled. "What is step two?"

He refrained from pumping his fist. "Dinner."

"I'm all dressed and ready to go, but I have one condition."

"Let's hear it." He crossed his arms over his chest and waited.

Jennifer sighed. "I don't want you to ever be jealous on my behalf." She tilted her head as if egging him to refute her.

"Agreed."

"And—"

"You said one."

She glared at him. "Do you want to go to dinner or not?"

He nodded and pressed his lips together.

"I won't pretend that the things you said this morning didn't hurt me."

"I know and I feel bad for saying it. You see, when things get really tight, I say anything that comes to mind. I hope you can forgive me."

"I want you to stop pushing me away."

Unbelievable! Don't ask for much, do ya?

He bobbed his head. "Five minutes?" he asked.

"Take your time. I'm not going anywhere." She looked away, but not before he saw the twinkle in her eyes.

Muttering under his breath, he hurried to wash his face and change his clothes.

Whoa! Am I going on a real honest-to-goodness date?

He couldn't help but smile at his reflection, loving the idea of a night out with Jennifer. He fixed his eye patch and patted his growing hair. The beanie seemed out of place with his black shirt. He tugged it off and checked his inner disgust meter.

His blond hair had grown relatively long, and the skin on his left cheek was turning pink.

Not too bad if the restaurant lights are dim.

He pushed the strands behind his ears and picked up his keys from the bureau.

"Let me feed Drew and let him out before we go," he said as he passed by the living room and whistled.

"I fed him earlier," Jennifer answered from the kitchen.

"What are you doing up?" His voice turned harsh.

Jennifer turned from the sink and held up her hand in a warning gesture. "I'm using the crutches so there is no undue pressure on the foot. Besides, I wanted my flowers in a vase."

"I don't have a vase."

"I know. I improvised." She held up a glass pitcher filled with the blooms and laughed.

He grinned, unable to resist her charm. "Ready?" He preceded her down the hall and opened the front door for her in an attempt to be a perfect gentleman.

Lancaster offered few choices for fine dining so he'd decided to drive to the neighboring town of Palmdale. The town boasted restaurants that were a step above fast food places or hole-in-the-wall eateries.

After driving for a few miles, he exited the freeway and located the popular restaurant row frequented by locals.

"What are you in the mood for?" he asked.

"Anything is fine with me."

"Italian?"

"Sure."

Being a weeknight, the place wasn't as packed as he imagined it was on any given weekend. They were shown a cozy booth with ambient lighting and plenty of privacy. Just the way he wanted. Once Jennifer was seated, he opted for the space next to her.

"This place is beautiful. Have you been here before?" she asked, glancing around appreciatively.

He shook his head. "This is my first time." The place was nice and appealing, but nothing compared to the woman next to him. "Would you like a glass of wine?"

She shook her head. "I'm still taking pain pills. I don't think it's good to mix them." She turned to look at him.

"True. I guess we'll be toasting with water tonight." He raked his fingers through his hair, feeling self-conscious all of a sudden.

Jennifer continued to watch him. "You know, I like you without a beanie. I can see your face better."

He grimaced. "I have to get out of the hot thing from time to time." He looked away, not sure if he wanted the attention.

Jennifer tugged at his arm until he was looking directly at her. "Your eyes have always been so expressive and full of depth. It's like staring at an abstract painting."

He focused on her face and breathed deep. "I have one left, so that depth is kinda screwed right now. I can tell you this, though: you look spectacular tonight." His cheeks ached as Jennifer blushed and his grin stretched even wider across his face.

Their little exchange was halted when the waiter appeared, smiling and pad in hand, for their drink and appetizer orders.

"As I was saying, you're exquisite, but I'm sure you know that already." He decided to pour it thick, and he took her hand and lifted it to his lips for a kiss.

Jennifer took on a deep cherry hue while she squirmed under his touch.

Although she let him keep holding her hand, he sensed that, just like him, she wanted to shift the attention away from herself.

"Tell me, what do you intend to do after your treatment?"

He scowled out of habit but remembered that he was on best behavior watch. He leaned against the leather cushion and sighed.

Might as well come clean.

"I've never thought about it."

"Why?"

He glanced sideways at her, tilting his head slightly. "Do you have a questionnaire with you?"

She giggled. "Actually, I had them memorized, and you didn't answer my question."

He turned her palm up and trailed his fingers across the lines while he searched for the right things to say. "Well, before I enlisted, I had a degree in music. I always dreamt of writing music, and playing in front of a crowd." He started strumming an imaginary chord inside her hand.

"You still have that degree, right?"

He narrowed his eyes and nodded.

"I don't see why anything should stop you from doing what you wanted."

Blake had to hand it to her. Jennifer was a woman who said things as she saw them. Just like Trent had described her.

"I don't see how I can play around people and not make them uncomfortable." He gestured to his face.

"There isn't anything there that repulses me." She pulled her hand from his and traced her fingers along his damaged cheek. "I think the eye patch gives you a mysterious air, and it's sexy."

Mysterious?

Sexy?

Okay, now that's not awkward.

The very thing he abhorred, she found sexy?

"I don't know what to say to that," he said, pulling her hand away from his face.

"Say that you'll think about writing songs and playing for me."

Blake stared at her in disbelief.

Was she really asking him to do the one thing he dreaded to do? And what good would it do? He'd start hoping for more, and that would lead to embarrassment and potential disappointment.

"Am I one of the causes you're championing? Getting a down-and-out vet into circulation again?"

Jennifer jutted her chin in her familiar display of stubbornness, and then nodded. "Yes. You have no business hiding at home."

Blake felt a hint of irritation rise, but before he could lash out at her, the server arrived with their drinks, a basket of focaccia bread, and dipping oil. The server left with their entrée orders, buying Blake more time to compose himself. A good thing, since he was tired of being angry.

If the woman would just stop hitting so close to home.

For the next few minutes, they busied themselves with the antipasto.

After he had taken a few bites, Blake wiped his mouth with the dinner napkin and faced her. "I'm not hiding. I just don't see how easy it would be to rejoin the world after what I saw in the battlefield and the people I have killed. The guilt is not easy to live with."

This was the most he'd said to anyone about returning from active duty with a career-ending injury. It felt good to get it off his chest, but it also left him in unchartered territory of being weak and exposed.

—⁓—

Jennifer watched Blake lower his gaze and close his eye.

An unfamiliar ache shot through her heart for all that he had gone through. She saw the anguish in his face and heard the suffering in his voice. What had this man seen out there for him to come home broken and feeling like he had nothing else to offer?

She bit her lip to keep from tearing up. She choked a sob and swallowed hard.

Their entrees came and put further discussion on hold.

She had lost her appetite but pretended to eat by shoving the pasta around her plate. Throwing desperate glances at Blake, she kept tabs on his progress. After eating half, he had started doing the same thing with his chicken parmigiana.

Blake summoned the waiter for a refill of his water, took a deep breath, and picked up her hand after the long and tense silence. "It's terrifying to discover that after eight years in the service the rest of the world has moved on without me, without us. I don't know how to act around people anymore. I feel alienated, and that is not just others' doing but my own, too.

It's difficult to forget the faces; the lives I took, the ones taken from me. Nothing feels the same. I don't understand it when people tell me I'm lucky to be alive. I only have one eye. When I'm in an unfamiliar place, I bump into things. I have a limp that might not ever go away, and I . . . it's all so messed up."

Jennifer absorbed his emotions as if they were her own and found a newfound respect and compassion for the man. Just like Trent, Blake had seen enough atrocities in the field to give him a lifetime of nightmares and sleepless nights, but to let him dwell on what he had lost and his limitations was a great disservice.

She lifted his chin with her free hand until he was looking at her. "Have you talked to someone about your feelings?"

"Talk to a shrink?"

She nodded. Certainly the stigma of speaking to a specialist could scare anyone back into his cave.

His jaw pulsed, and she felt his tension at her fingertips. "I don't need anyone to tell me that I'm not the only one who feels this way."

"Blake, listen to me. Refusing to talk is the one thing keeping you stuck. You have *so* much to live for. I'm not an expert, and I won't tell you how to live your life. I just want to see you try to be happy."

"Why?" His voice was low and husky.

No point lying.

She held his gaze, unwavering. "Because I care for you."

"Since when?"

She sighed and summoned the strength to go on. "The moment we first . . ."

"Aren't you in the least bit disgusted by my appearance?"

Shaking her head, Jennifer closed her eyes for a brief moment. When she reopened them, they were filled with tears. "And I've never once felt pity. You have enough of it for yourself."

"What about Trent?"

She took a deep breath, deciding that, once and for all, Blake had to know her true feelings. "I love him. I still do, but not in the same way he did me. He was my protector and best friend, and I'm grateful for our friendship. When he proposed, I didn't have the heart to say no. I agreed to marry him for the wrong reason. I felt guilty. I was planning to tell him the truth the next time he returned, but I never got the chance."

Blake inhaled a sharp breath, twined their fingers, and lifted them to his mouth, kissing the back of her hand. "I have nothing to offer anyone. Damaged goods don't do well in relationships these days."

"I'm not asking you for anything but to give yourself a chance to live again, and to quit hiding behind your injuries. Allow me to help you."

"What can you possibly do for me?"

A breath of hope sluiced through her veins. "I can start by going with you to your appointment tomorrow."

He stared at her. "What appointment?"

"With the eye specialist."

Blake closed his good eye and shook his head. "I don't know about that."

"It's your call. I'm just here as a cheering squad."

He laughed a brittle sound that cracked with emotion. "What would this cheering cost me?"

"Nothing, except your word that you won't shut me out. No more Mr. Grumpy."

He opened his eye and focused on her, offering a small smile. "Promises, promises. I'll see what I can do."

Not bad at all.

In truth, his word was good enough for her. With Blake, taking one step forward meant being prepared to take two steps back. It would be challenging and also disconcerting, but she believed he was worth it.

"Hey, wake up!" Jennifer whispered in Blake's ear.

He stirred. "Hmm . . ."

She touched his shoulder and gave him a gentle nudge. "Blake, you've got a doctor's appointment, remember?"

Blake peeled his eye wide, and his first reaction was to reach for the patch on his nightstand. When his hand hit nothing but air, he bolted upright, covering the socket where his eye used to be. When he felt the leather cover in place, he sagged back down.

She knelt down next to him with a worried expression. "I wouldn't have come in if you weren't wearing your patch."

"I don't appreciate being surprised."

"I'm sorry. I didn't mean to make you uncomfortable."

"You always make me uncomfortable." The sting in his proclamation was hard to ignore.

Here we go again.

She took a deep breath and touched his shoulder. "Okay, let's stop this. I'm getting sick of you running hot and cold on me."

Her heart tripped a little. His bouts of crankiness were understandable.

As much as she wanted to coddle Blake, she knew she had to play a tough role to keep him focused on himself and not on his misgivings.

"Then stay out of this room." He glared at her.

She crossed her arms over her chest, and glared back. "And if I don't?"

With a sudden movement, he snaked a hand around her waist and pulled her to him. She almost stumbled, but he kept her steady. "You're going to get this," he said before seizing her mouth in an urgent kiss.

She stared at him, dumbfounded, her lips tingling.

Blake got to his feet and offered her a hand. "It's about time I left you speechless." This time, his deep chuckle reverberated around the room. He held her shoulders tight and pivoted them to face the door. He leaned toward her neck and grazed his lips across her skin. "Be a good girl and wait for me outside."

And like a good girl, Jennifer left the guest room, still reeling. If he kept this up, her resolve to keep things light between them would mean nothing.

She went back to his bedroom and sat on the bed while listening closely to the sounds of him moving around the other room.

The ever-changing emotions that Blake had been exhibiting spelled trouble. She wasn't looking for a quick romp, but she couldn't figure out where the teasing and flirting was going to lead them.

What do you want from him?

The answer came back in a rush. She wanted more, but her pride wouldn't let her ask. She knew she wouldn't be able to the handle rejection . . . not again.

Distracted, she reached into her duffel bag and retrieved a pair of denim pants and a pink cotton T-shirt.

If Blake didn't want her to see the eye specialist, then she'd ask him to drop her off at a hotspot for a better Internet reception. It was a lie, but time away from him, no matter how short, would give her an opportunity to sort her head out.

When she stepped out, all dressed and carrying her laptop bag, the inviting aroma of coffee wafted from the kitchen.

"Jenny, a healthy breakfast is waiting for you."

Kill me now!

Trent had been around all her life and he was predictable, in a good and comfortable way. This situation with Blake was complicated. With limited knowledge about the man and what he'd gone through, she was scared this was heartbreak waiting to happen.

Jennifer placed her laptop bag on the table and went to the kitchen, where a bowl of cereal topped with slices of bananas and strawberries was waiting.

Blake turned, smiling. "If we eat fast enough, we can still make it on time." He gestured to her chair, sat down with two cups of coffee, and slid one in front of her.

Death by whiplash.

"What made you change your mind?" she asked.

"Milk?"

She nodded. "Are you ignoring my question?"

"I want to," he said, while pouring the milk onto her cereal. "Say when."

"When."

He filled his bowl and began eating, seemingly oblivious to the expectant look on her face.

"We have ten minutes left," he mumbled between bites.

Exasperated, she ate as fast as she could. As she nursed her coffee, Blake broke the thick silence.

"I figured I should go. I don't have to wear it if I don't like it. It can be sort of a special occasion accessory." The smile he gave her failed to reach his eye.

Jennifer kept checking on Blake, gauging his mood. He'd been quiet since they'd left, and the silence made her jittery. To calm her nerves, she concentrated on the rock music playing on the radio and the air brushing the soft cover of the Jeep. The problem of knowing only bits and pieces about his life made it difficult to guess how he'd react to certain questions or even ideas.

He gave her a quick sideways glance. "You can quit staring at me. I'm fine, if that's what you're wondering about."

"How can you tell I'm looking at you?" She scrutinized him.

"You may be in my blind spot, but my hearing is pretty damn good. I can hear your slightest movement, your body shifting, and your back rubbing the upholstery while you twitch around over there watching me. Not to mention, the gears turning in your head. You're squeaking." He chuckled.

Unbelievable.

She turned to face the windshield and stared straight ahead. Blake was going to test her patience, and he'd be surprised to find out that she wouldn't be easily put off.

They arrived for his appointment with plenty of time to spare. The receptionist greeted them with a cursory smile and handed Blake a clipboard of papers.

Jennifer glanced around the room.

A few of the patients waiting seemed to have similar ailments as Blake. Although most of them wore dark sunglasses, Blake seemed to be the only one who preferred an eye patch.

After he finished filling out the necessary paperwork, they sat in silence.

———

Who am I kidding?

The more he picked on Jennifer, teasing her, criticizing her for caring, the more he fell in love with her. He wasn't good at expressing his feelings, and he'd ended up looking like an ass anyway.

Then why am I so anxious?

The clear answer was his inability to believe that it wasn't pity that drove her closer to him. He would rather stick to his silly notions than admit to himself that there was a spark between them. The changes in his appearance and the uncertainty of his future crippled his belief that a woman would ever be interested in him. And this visit to the doctor had been more for her sake than his.

"Mr. Connor?" the receptionist called out his name.

Blake stood, the thought of someone poking his sightless eye and fitting him with a cosmetic replacement causing his steps to falter. He left Jennifer without saying a word, intent on keeping the mask on to salvage his flagging pride.

The receptionist led Blake to a nondescript room with nothing but posters of satisfied patients in their before and after pictures. He kept a stony face as he raked his lone eye over each and every poster.

"Please have a seat, and the doctor will be right in," the woman said.

Blake nodded and moved toward the chair to wait.

A fake eye so I can be a fake normal guy? This is a mistake.

The door opened and a gruff looking gentleman entered carrying a large briefcase.

Blake eyed the attaché and wondered what it contained.

"Mr. Connor, I'm Dr. Dent."

Blake grunted a response, not certain he was up to a full-blown conversation, but shook the man's hand anyway.

Besides, I'm not here to talk but to get a goddamn eyeball.

The doctor sat on a round black stool and scooted it close to Blake's chair. His expression was inscrutable as he assessed Blake's eye patch. "I see you prefer the patch to wearing sunglasses. I like that."

Blake stared at the man, unsure how to interpret the unsolicited comment. "Excuse me?"

The doctor chuckled and without any warning, he reached for his right eye and removed the shell.

Blake jumped out of his chair and slammed into the wall. "What the hell?" he asked, feeling like he was in some sort of twilight zone. The doctor gestured for him to sit, but Blake remained standing, ready to bolt if the weirdness scale tipped any farther.

"I felt the same way when I lost mine from eye disease. I refused to hide under dark-colored lenses. I wanted everyone to know that I was missing an eye. Besides, my girlfriend thought it was sexy. Sexy enough she agreed to be my wife." Dr. Dent replaced the shell, smiled, and winked.

Jennifer's face when she'd mentioned the patch being sexy over dinner flashed before Blake.

Man, I'm not even going there.

He slid back into the chair, still smarting from the shock. "I bet that gets your patients climbing the wall every time you pull that stunt."

Dr. Dent laughed and urged him closer. "It works all the time. It lets my patients know I can relate."

The doctor appeared to be in his midfifties, with a potbelly and receding hairline. It was hard not to warm to his unorthodox manner. Blake found himself easing up a little, but still on guard should Dent decide to do another striptease on him.

"Relax, my boy." Dr. Dent said, as if reading his mind. "I understand that the circumstance surrounding your eye loss is somewhat different from mine. I won't nag you for details, but I do want to know why you refuse to wear one."

Blake thought about the question.

In a way, the patch had become his badge of honor and showed that he had done what had been asked of him and that everything he had seen and endured had been real, not just a figment of his imagination. If there was a precious lesson the war had taught him, it was that he was as good as the next soldier, injured or not. The rest was up to him to try and fit back into the society he'd bled for.

"I don't need an accessory," Blake said.

"And yet you're here," the doctor said in a kind voice. "Something or someone must have inspired you." It wasn't a question but an observation from a man who had likely heard every possible excuse there was from his patients.

"You could say that," he admitted, thinking of Jennifer.

"What's important is that you're here." The doctor gave him a triumphant smile before scooting over to open the briefcase and reveal a wide array of prosthetic shells in different sizes and colors of irises.

Blake felt sick to his stomach. The idea of fitting something foreign into his body seemed so wrong.

Dr. Dent glanced at his disgusted face and offered a reassuring smile.

"All I ask is that you adopt a sense of humor. You've got nothing to lose."

"You aren't the first to ask," he muttered, eyeing the shell the man had picked out. It was slightly smaller than the others, with a blue iris painted on it.

"This is one of my favorite jokes. When your children are in another room, and you want them to behave, leave the prosthetic eye on the table and tell them you're watching them." Dr. Dent laughed.

Blake lifted an eyebrow and shrugged. He couldn't imagine ever having kids. Not because he didn't want kids, but his appearance would scare his future ex-wife away.

You have Jennifer.

He shook his head at the thought.

"I need you to remove the patch so I can see which of these fits best."

Reluctantly, Blake slipped the patch off his head but kept his eyes closed. There was no gaping hole where his eye had been. Instead, a pink piece of flesh was in place. It wasn't horrifying to look at, but it wasn't a sight to behold either.

"I need to check your socket in order to find the right fit for you." Dr. Dent's voice nudged him from the sea of awkwardness he was swimming in.

Blake opened his eye and stared straight ahead, unable to meet the doctor's gaze. There was a slight pressure as Dr. Dent fitted the first one then tried another. Through the next several minutes, Blake kept his expression stoic.

The doctor recited the process of creating his prosthetic eye, while jotting down some notes and measurements.

After the procedure was over, the doctor asked him to come back for another fitting of the new shell.

His anxiety began to diminish when he stepped into the waiting room and Jennifer looked up from her magazine.

"Is everything okay?" she asked.

Blake responded with a curt nod, walked straight to the door, and held it open for her.

Jennifer gathered her crutches from the floor and followed him.

He maintained a faster pace, not interested in discussing the appointment or his concerns.

An uncomfortable silence lingered during the drive back, but Jennifer seemed to be respecting his unspoken request for quiet.

He glanced at her, only to find her staring into space and chewing her bottom lip, and his mouth watered at the memory of tasting her sweet mouth again.

Damn, Connor! Get your thoughts out of your pants.

When he turned on the deserted stretch of his street, he saw an unfamiliar car parked by his house. Slowing down as they passed the black luxury sports car, he took note of the car's license plate before easing into the driveway.

"Stay here," he said, and slid out the driver's seat.

"What's going on?"

"Just stay here and lock the doors."

Blake approached the car with caution and tried to see who was driving, but the glare of the sun reflecting off the windshield made it impossible to see inside. With prudence, he tapped on the glass on the driver's side.

The window rolled down and a man stuck his head out. "Hi, is that Jennifer with you?"

The man wasn't your average guy-next-door type. This one was wearing a dark suit, a pretty boy smile, and had sparkling blue eyes.

And Blake instantly disliked him. "Who wants to know?"

The door opened and the man stood up, towering over him. "I'm Matt. I'm here to check on her." Matt offered his hand.

Blake ignored the outstretched hand and turned around.

Here to check on her?

He heard footsteps behind him but he kept walking.

"Is she all right?" Matt asked.

"See for yourself."

"Matthew!" Jennifer's muffled voice from the confines of the Jeep made his blood boil. She waved at Matt.

Rushing past him, Matt scuttled to the passenger side and wrapped an arm around Jennifer's waist. "Hey! I've missed you," Matt said.

Pretty Boy planted an affectionate kiss on Jennifer's cheek, and Blake's chest tightened. Unable to stay and watch, he hurried inside, ignoring Drew's excited barking as he marched out to the backyard and flopped into one of the patio chairs. Removing himself had been the only way to guarantee Mr. Pretty Boy lived a minute longer.

Jennifer's excitement upon seeing Matt mixed with worry at Blake's sudden dark mood. From the corner of her eye, she saw him stalk inside the house.

"Congratulations, girl! I always knew you could do it." Matt twirled her around.

Jennifer laughed despite the unease that settled in her chest. "Thanks!" She glanced toward the front door, wanting to check on Blake. The way he had avoided her question after his appointment had raised warning bells.

Matt lowered her on the ground. "What's wrong? You don't look so happy."

"You seem to forget that Cinderella's not one hundred percent yet." She gestured to her bandaged foot.

"Then why don't I carry the princess to her castle, then?"

"Put me down." She landed a playful slap on his shoulder but Matt continued to carry her.

She stopped her giggling once they walked inside the quiet house.

Matt put her down on the sofa, and she heard Drew bark from the other side of the sliding door.

His lips were pulled into a nasty snarl, exposing his long sharp teeth, and his attention was completely focused on Matt.

She heard Blake reprimand him, and the dog sat on his heels right away, his eyes remaining locked on her guest.

Matt chuckled and returned his attention to her. "What's wrong with the dog's boss? He seems upset."

Jennifer shared her friend's sentiment, but didn't want to admit it. She glanced toward the patio again, hoping to catch a glimpse of Blake.

Matt narrowed his eyes. "I think it's best if we go someplace where we can talk, and I can eat without the dog eyeing me like I'm dinner."

There was no fooling Matt. They'd known each other long enough that things rarely escaped each other's notice anymore.

"Let me tell Blake real quick," she said, and hopped her way toward the patio door.

The air was already stifling, and she wondered if it was even advisable for Blake to be outdoors in such punishing heat. It was good that Matt suggested they talk elsewhere so Blake wouldn't have to feel put out in his own home.

"Blake?"

He threw her a dark glare. "What?"

Okay. So he's upset.

"I'm going to step out with Matt for a b—"

"You don't have to ask for my permission," he said, his expression turning blank.

She had thought informing him was a good idea instead of just slipping away. Then again, she was beginning to realize she apparently never knew the right thing to do as far as Blake was concerned.

"What is it this time, Blake? Is this about me pushing you to go to the doctor? Or are you just in a bad mood for no reason whatsoever? I'm getting sick and tired of your long face and grumpy attitude."

Their gaze met and only the dog's heavy panting broke the tension-filled silence.

"I'm sorry for taking my frustrations out on you," Blake said in a quiet voice filled with remorse.

"Fine. We'll talk when I get back."

She watched as Blake opened his mouth, seeming to deliberate on what to say, but closed it instead. He nodded and looked away.

"I have my cell phone if you need anything." She stepped back inside and found Matt seated on the sofa. "Let's go." No doubt, he'd overheard everything he needed to form an opinion she knew she'd hear about later.

Once inside his luxurious car, Matt chuckled. "I never thought I'd see the day when you felt the heat of being in love."

Jennifer let his words sit while she pondered Blake's abrupt mood change.

They arrived at a small Mexican bar and grill.

"They claim to have the best fajita in town." Matt pointed to the sign outside the establishment.

Seated at a table for four and their food order taken, Matt produced a thick wad of papers from his briefcase and spread them across the table. "I've gone through them with a fine-tooth comb, but I still want you to look them over just in case. Everything you asked for has been included."

Jennifer leafed through each page, reading specifics and skimming over the boilerplate details until she came across one condition from the company that wanted her ready-to-wear creations. "What does working closely with their models mean?"

Matt smiled apologetically. "That is the one nonnegotiable condition."

"In plain English, please."

Matt hesitated.

From her experience working with him, this meant trouble.

"Well, given that you're a new designer, they want you to drop by with your samples to try them on their own models as often as possible."

"Why can't they send home a model with me?"

How difficult is it to provide me with one of their precious mannequins?

"We're talking about live ones, darling." He laughed when her eyebrows shot up.

"I can't make that daily commute, Matt. That's seventy miles, one way." She shook her head. The I-14 was a long stretch of nothing, and enough to drive a daily commuter to tears.

Matt quoted an exorbitant offer and Jennifer gaped.

When she'd entered this trade, her main focus had been to see her work sold in stores. She had never thought that a large compensation would accompany such an endeavor.

"With their fat offer, you can rent a loft or even a one bedroom apartment and still have enough left to go on vacation every other month."

The possibility left her reeling. This was her dream coming true.

But what about Blake?

Yeah, what about him?

"What are you worried about?" Matt leaned closer. "Don't bother answering. I'm going to put my money on Captain Hook."

She landed a good-natured slap on his shoulder. "No name-calling please."

"It's that dude, huh?" He leaned back in his seat and clasped his hands together behind his head.

She sighed. "Should I even attempt to lie?"

"Humor me?" He chuckled.

"Well, he's a big, bad grouch. He snaps when I offer help. He kisses me to shut me up. It's a weird relationship so far. I'm not even sure it's a relationship because we can't seem to agree on even the simplest things."

Matt leaned on the table and took her hand. "My dear child. That is what we call foreplay. I'm sure you've heard of it?"

Unbelievable.

For some insane reason it was easier to talk to Matt, since Coleen tended to be overly cautious. "It's tough because he'll let me in, and just when I think we're gaining ground, he'll blast me off."

"And you let that deter you?"

She shook her head, feeling miserable.

"Good. Because the Jennifer Owens I know doesn't let anything or anyone stop her."

The food arrived, giving her a chance to focus on business and weigh the conditions surrounding the contract.

Matt ate while she sipped on her iced tea.

She would be a fool to pass this once-in-a-lifetime chance to make a name for herself in the fashion world. And Blake, well, she shouldn't hold her breath where the man was concerned. She was certain that this thing between her and Blake would sort itself out when the right time came.

"Give me a pen," she said in a rush.

Matt stopped mid-bite and grinned. "You don't waste time, do you?" He put down his fajita, wiped his hands on the napkin, and produced a pen from his suit pocket.

"I've been waiting for this opportunity. I don't think luck will knock on my door twice." With trembling fingers, she affixed her signature on the document and shoved it back toward Matt. "Put it away before I change my mind."

Her phone rang, and Jennifer glanced at a number she didn't recognize. "Jennifer Owens."

"Ms. Owens, Officer Cortez here."

"Oh, hi. I hope you have some good news for me," she said, gesturing at Matt to wait.

"Actually, I do. The fingerprints we have got from your place matched a set of fingerprints from another break-in at a convenience store in Palmdale. We have the guy in custody. I will call you with more information in the next few days. If your window has been replaced, I think it would be safe for you to go back there."

"That's fantastic! Thank you so much."

Now that she could return home, Jennifer wasn't sure how to approach Blake with the news. Another potential outburst could be expected.

After the meal, she had Matt drive her to her house where work on the broken window had already started, and Mr. Smith was supervising the workers.

Her good neighbor waved once he spotted her.

"I'll wait here. I need to call and let them know about your acceptance, anyway." Matt pulled out his shiny cell phone.

Jennifer bobbed her head, still reeling at the idea of packing up and leaving the place she had called home for years. Los Angeles wasn't a bad place to live—a tad busy for her liking—but a daily commute was out of the question.

"They should be done soon." Mr. Smith gestured toward the two men from the window company as she approached. "I also had your locks changed." He jingled several keys on a ring.

"Thank you." Jennifer surveyed her property and felt an overwhelming desire to renege on the newly signed contract. "I'm going to close this place up during the week, and will be back on weekends."

Mr. Smith studied her with his sharp gray eyes. "You landed the contract, didn't you?"

She nodded. "I'm torn about living in the city."

"You'll be fine. Call me if you need anything." He placed a weathered hand on her shoulder and patted.

Jennifer looked around the place and felt another pang of sadness.

She and Mr. Smith chatted for a bit while watching the men at work before she returned to the car to find Matt finishing his phone call.

"Okay, they're ready for you to start next week. Will you be up to working with that foot of yours?" Matt shifted the car into drive and hit the gas pedal.

"The wound is healing, and as long as I walk in flats, I should be fine." The problem wasn't her foot, but a certain man who might not take her news lightly. "Thanks, Matt. I'll call you tonight."

Matt stopped in front of Blake's house, and she climbed out of the car.

"Do you need help moving some of your stuff?" he asked.

She shook her head without looking back. The only thing she needed was additional backup in case Blake went berserk.

—◦◦◦—

Blake stared at nothing in particular, still seated in the patio chair long after he heard Pretty Boy's car speed away.

The bastard kissed her and held her.

This whole green-eyed monster thing was so unlike him. In the past, this type of situation wouldn't have affected him, but with Matt all he wanted to do was knock him on his ass for even looking at Jennifer.

The trouble was he wasn't sure he believed she was interested in him, despite her responses to his kisses. Heat suffused his body when the vision of their twined limbs flashed in his mind. The woman had no idea how she affected him. Sex for him was pleasurable, a way to satiate a man's need, but with Jennifer everything he knew went out the window. This went beyond physical attraction. He wanted to possess not just her body but her heart and soul as well. This shit with Matt had him trying to come to terms with an overwhelming need to strangle any man who came near her, let alone touched her.

He had made a promise, though. He had to find a way to shove his jealousy aside and keep the monster at bay. He had to keep his end of the bargain.

He decided a cold shower was the answer for not only his hot temper but also the hard-on he'd been sporting more often than not these days.

Blake was grilling the last steak when Drew's bark alerted him to Jennifer's arrival. Plastering on a forced smile, he went inside to greet her while trying to hide the uncertainties and insecurities that had his insides tied in a knot.

The grin on Jennifer's face made him pause, and the image of her and Matt crept through his mind. It took a tremendous amount of restraint not to scowl.

Don't go there, Connor.

"Hungry?" Blake asked, watching her lithe movement with narrowed eyes.

She's even walking better.

"Yes. What are we having?"

"I'm grilling some steaks." He pointed at the papers she'd left on the coffee table. "What are those?"

"The contract I signed."

"Oh."

"Need any help?"

"Just the plates and stuff. The steaks are done."

They had each fixed a plate and settled at the table before Blake gave in to his curiosity.

"Tell me about the contract."

Jennifer finished chewing and took a big gulp of her soda. "Well, before I do that, let me tell you about my house. Officer Cortez called. The fingerprints they found matched some from break-ins in the area. They caught the guy, so he said it should be safe for me to go home, and Mr. Smith has taken care of the window and the locks."

He couldn't seem to swallow the big lump in his throat. "What are your plans?"

"I'm going to go back tonight so I can clean up and pack some of my things."

I knew this was too good to be true.

His gut twisted with dread. "Then what?"

"The contract demands I spend time with the client's models, and I have to find a place in the city during the week so I don't have to drive back and forth."

He didn't even try to hide his dismay.

"What?" he asked, clenching his teeth until his jaw shook. He'd heard her, but couldn't process the ludicrous idea.

"I have to find a place in LA before the week is over."

And just like that, Jennifer was walking out of his life.

Suddenly, the steak tasted like plastic, and he found it difficult to swallow the darn thing. With disgust, he dropped the fork and knife, and his appetite went AWOL on him. All he could do was stare at her, knowing that he had failed on so many levels. He'd driven her to leave, and now she was moving away. Who knew if Pretty Boy would be warming her bed at night?

Damn it!

Jennifer's hand wound up on top of his that was clenched on the table. "Hey, what's wrong?"

"Nothing. I'm not hungry anymore." He stood up and gathered his plate. Looking at the rare meat, he threw the uneaten scrap to Drew, who gobbled the thick piece with gusto.

"Where are you going?"

"To my room."

Blake grabbed the dusty tequila bottle from the counter on his way to his room. He pivoted while unscrewing the lid, but Jennifer had followed him and closed her fingers around the bottle, trying to pry it away from his grasp.

"What are you doing?" He flared his nostrils and tugged the glass jug back in his direction.

"You're not going to drink. You will tell me what's going on. Just remember the last time you turned to alcohol."

I wish I could.

"Stop telling me what to do! You're going to leave, and I'm going to do what I damn well please."

Jennifer took a step back, pulling the bottle from him. "Where is this coming from, Blake? You can talk to me."

"What do you want me to say? That I'm fucking jealous? That I don't want you to go? C'mon, Jennifer, I know damn well you're going to do what you want, no matter what I say." He gritted his teeth. This talking shit was not his style.

I'm scared. Can't you tell? I'm scared shitless of losing you, of the things I can't control.

A smile graced her lips, which only added to his aggravation. "I can't believe you're jealous of Matt," she whispered.

Blake groaned with exasperation and fled to his room, but Jennifer trailed right behind him.

And now you're laughing at me. Great!

She placed the tequila on top of the nightstand, walked up to him and placed her palms on his chest.

"I think this is what we both need."

She lifted her mouth to his and caressed his lips.

Confusion battled with desire, and he was powerless to stop himself from the deluge of warmth she elicited. He returned her kiss with fervor and applied pressure on her back to draw her closer.

Jennifer closed her eyes.

Tremors rocked him as her body rubbed against his, prepping him for action.

"I like being close to you." The words came out rough, sounding shaken.

"Me, too, Blake. Me, too." Her voice was low and seductive, and she threaded her fingers through his hair while his tongue pushed its way into her parted lips. The warmth of her mouth was inviting.

Mixed with her pleasing feminine scent, his senses were caught in a whirlwind of desire.

Jennifer circled her tongue in his mouth, stroking the insides.

He pressed her body closer to his. Tracing his hand on her thighs, he worked its way up to the curve of her body. He was aching for her.

"I want . . . to . . . ." She moaned softly and gasped. ". . . ah, Blake . . . I want to make love to you." Jennifer clenched her hand tighter in his hair while she arched her body harder into his.

Blake stiffened. There was nothing more he would rather do at this moment than to make her his.

Can I risk it? Should I?

He couldn't very well consummate their love fully clothed. This was Jennifer, not some woman that he could just jerk around. He wanted to pleasure her in every way possible, but the thought of revealing his disfigured body to her made him want to run and hide.

She deserves better than me.

He pushed her away and raked his fingers through his hair then turned away to hide his frustration.

"No. Don't do that! Don't pull away from me." She was still breathless from their kisses.

"There's nothing else I would rather do . . ." His voice sounded pained and defeated, and pathetic. He faced her. "I want it more than anything in this world, but I—" He couldn't say the words.

"I don't understand." Jennifer furrowed her brows and confusion marred her beautiful face. He longed to smooth the lines away.

"I'm not ready to show . . ." He gestured to his body. "I can't."

"I won't pretend it doesn't exist, but it's not what makes you special, Blake." She jabbed at his chest. "The beating heart underneath is what's important to me. Your scars mean one thing to me, that you're a fighter. Can you trust me enough to share this moment with me?"

The T word was overrated, but the ache between his legs was dictating. If he threw caution to the wind just this once, he'd have the chance to hold the woman he'd loved for so long and a memory to last him a lifetime.

As if sensing the inner battle raging within him, Jennifer rubbed his back with her palm. Even with the layer of clothing that separated them, he felt her warmth.

"We go nice and slow." The sincerity in her voice encouraged him to hope.

Giving in to his intense need to take a part of her with him, Blake carried her to his bed and ignored the warning signals in his head.

"Promise me you'll stop me if you can't bear it. I'll understand." His voice was barely more than a whisper. He was still unsure about the whole situation, but his self-control was hanging by a thread.

Blake dimmed the lights low, leaving nothing more than a soft glow of Jennifer's silhouette. He could still see her face in the darkened room, but the less she saw of him, the better off she was.

He walked to the console that housed his CD player, and flicked the power on. "Cause We've Ended as Lovers" filled the room.

He sighed slowly, still unsure, and while the battle raged within him, Blake eased his body next to Jennifer's. Tracing his fingertips along the softness of her cheek, he closed his mouth on hers with urgency this time, trying not to think of the outcome.

Jennifer returned his kisses with an enthusiasm that left him believing— in himself, in her, in the possibility of them.

Blake broke the kiss and moved his mouth down her jawline, caressing her neck with his tongue.

She arched her body in response, meeting his languid caress of her skin. She dug her fingers into the small of his back, gently scraping his skin with her fingernails. The sensation of her touch, coupled with the inviting sound of her whimpers, amplified his senses into a spiraling wave of lust.

Blake intensified his tongue's teasing on her skin, intent on keeping her moaning with pleasure.

Jennifer wrapped her legs around his hips the moment he lowered himself on top, to meld their bodies together.

"I want to see you. All of you."

Jennifer nodded, and he slid her tank top over her head, exposing a delicate pink bra edged with black lace.

"Can you be any more perfect?" With trembling hands, he proceeded to strip her jeans and reveal a matching bikini that showed off her breathtaking curves. Blake devoured her almost naked figure, running his gaze from her breasts down to the arch of her waistline. He unstrapped her bra, displaying a pair of supple breasts that took his breath away. A primal moan slipped between his lips as he lowered his mouth and caressed her nipple with his tongue.

The surge of pleasure manifested from Jennifer's response when she curled underneath him, moaning in ecstasy. He let his tongue glide down her body, toward her belly button, while he held her waist with both hands and heaved his body onto hers. He felt her respond to his movement when she curved upward.

Jennifer tugged on his shirt. "Your clothes are in the way."

Fueled by lust, he wasted no time discarding his shirt and tossing it on the floor and stood before her with a need he'd been suppressing for a long time.

—⁓—

The strong contour of his half-naked body took Jennifer's breath away. She pushed to a sitting position and moved to the edge of the bed. His skin glistened with sweat in the glow of the modest light he had left for them.

Blake watched her while she traced her fingers from his jawline to his collarbone down to his chest muscles, where her hand rested. A tremor shook her body at the sight of him. Fear of scaring him away as she studied every dip and plane of his body guided her as she pounced into action before he regretted letting her in. She dragged her fingers across the expanse of his upper torso, and rested her eyes on the tattoo at the center of his broad chest.

"What is this?" She traced one finger along the shape of the body art.

"It's Trent's dog tag," he whispered.

"Why are you wearing his name?"

"It is a tribute to a brave man and a friend." His gaze was unwavering, so intense that she shuddered. When she didn't say a word, his voice was filled with uncertainty. "Am I disgusting you?"

Jennifer shook her head and spoke in a firm voice. "I love everything about you. This . . ." She traced a finger on the raised skin. "Is what makes you you. I would never ask for anything more." She lowered her mouth to kiss each scar, feeling his breath hitching with every touch of her lips.

He cupped her face and planted a kiss on her lips. "I want to be perfect for you."

"You are." She watched him closely as she pulled his jeans down to expose his boxers. She lowered her eyes to see the rest of him. Indeed, he had been wounded physically and was still dealing with the emotional aftermath. Her heart ached for him, but he was just as beautiful as she thought he would be. "You are perfect to me."

"Not as perfect as you are." Blake slid down on the bed next to her.

Emboldened, Jennifer pulled his boxers down. She settled on top of him and let her breasts rub against his skin as she inched down his body until she was face-to-face with his full arousal. Her breath quickened as she wrapped her mouth around the tip.

Blake gasped. "Sweet baby girl." He inched his hips upward.

She gently scraped her teeth against the skin of his erection. He grabbed a handful of her hair, and she took him deeper.

"I want to be inside you when I go."

She pulled away but not before she gave him a hard suck, unable to stop the bold smile when she heard him hiss in pleasure. "I'm all yours. You can do whatever you want."

Blake reached inside his drawer to produce a condom, and she watched while he quickly sheathed himself. Blake coaxed her closer and tugged off her panties. He let out a low whistle. "What did I do to deserve this?"

The wonder in his tone made her feel beautiful, wanted.

In one swift shift, he twisted their bodies until he was on top and cradled between her legs. A wicked grin teased his lips while his broad chest flexed as he penetrated her.

Jennifer's wetness allowed a gentle glide in. As her warmth wrapped him, the sound of their moans filled the room.

Blake thrust slowly at first, bracing his weight with his legs, while one hand teased the tight peak of her nipple. His breathing intensified with each push while she fought the urge to cry out in ecstasy.

"Don't hold it, I want to hear you," he whispered, pumping harder.

Watching his powerful jaw clench and the vein in his neck aroused Jennifer even more. Her high hit sooner than she'd hoped and a hoarse but satisfied cry tore out of her. During that moment, her world stopped spinning, and all she felt was the delicious suspension of total fulfillment.

She sighed quietly and smiled up at the beautiful man looking down. "Your turn," she murmured, shifting her body under his weight.

Blake chuckled and resumed thrusting.

Jennifer held his waist, feeling the muscles flexing with each shove. She clasped her legs around his hips and rode his wave, watching every emotion that flashed across his face.

"God!" Blake screamed and jerked.

A feeling of satisfaction blanketed her when she felt him tremble.

"Dear Jesus," he cried, and sent her into another climax again.

Blake collapsed on top of her, his breath coming in erratic bursts. She still felt him releasing seconds after he lay with his face buried in the crook of her neck.

When their breathing calmed, he lifted himself up, and she saw the contented smile that was no doubt showing on her face, too.

Blake couldn't brush the smile off his face. It had been plastered there ever since he'd woken up with Jennifer lying next to him in perfect, naked gloriousness.

She belongs here.

The thought kept repeating itself in his head, along with the feeling of invincibility that coursed through his veins, leaving him revitalized for the first time in a long while. He could get used to having her next to him in bed for all eternity.

The mere idea excited him. It had a nice ring to it.

"Damn!"

Jennifer stirred and twisted to face him. "Hmm?" A smile was etched on her lovely face.

"Nothing. Go back to sleep." He basked in the unique experience of not only feeling but seeing true happiness. The lines of worry were nowhere to be found across her brow, replaced instead by a contented expression that made her glow. It was difficult to believe he was responsible for it, but he hoped this wasn't the last time he saw it.

Blake glanced at his naked body, and the giddy feelings that had stayed with him all through the night evaporated into thin air. He saw flaps of repaired skin traveling from his chest down to his leg. The discolorations, patches, and puckered pink gouges seemed to be more obvious than ever in the morning light.

Stupid, idiotic!

He yanked the bedspread off, covered himself and hurried to the bathroom, picking up his discarded clothes from the floor in the process.

He stood under the shower, hoping the warm water would ease his anxiety.

It can't be.

Jennifer needed someone whole. She deserved a man who was comfortable in his own skin—someone who knew his worth and was unperturbed by insecurities and constant attacks of jealous fits.

He remained under the soothing spray of water until he felt a semblance of control.

By the time he stepped out of the shower, Jennifer was sitting at the counter in all her naked glory. His gaze instinctively traveled to her perky breasts and down to her beautiful center. As much as he wanted to stake claim on her after their wondrous night together, he wouldn't . . . not for selfish reasons.

Who am I fooling?

Jennifer looked at him with such a soft expression, her eyes so tender and her mouth . . .

Pity!

Blake felt like he was going to puke.

—∿∿∿—

Jennifer woke up with the urge to sing and cry out her happiness. What had happened the other night had been great, but last night had been different. Last night Blake had been fully aware and wholly participating.

This is what I've missed.

She reached out to where he'd slept but found nothing but empty space. She inhaled deep, letting his lingering scent saturate and tease her senses.

At the sound of the shower, Blake's naked body flashed in her mind, and Jennifer proceeded to the bathroom and sat on the counter, hoping to catch him off guard.

When Blake stepped out of the cubicle, there was no mistaking the contempt he threw in her direction.

Jennifer's gaze dropped to the towel that covered his body. She'd thought after they had made love that most of their issues would sort themselves out. "What's wrong, Blake?"

She couldn't understand how he saw himself as undesirable when all she wanted to do was go on a lovemaking marathon with this attractive and virile man.

Blake barely acknowledged her. Instead, he walked out of the bathroom and into the walk-in closet.

She followed like a lost puppy, unable to grapple with the sudden change in his mood.

"Nothing's wrong. I'm going to drive you home so you can get on with your life."

"What about last night?" she asked in a small voice.

Blake buttoned his fly and strode toward her with his bare chest in broad daylight. He stood before her, his blue eye sharp, unyielding. "Last night was great, but it's best to forget about it." His voice held no emotion, nothing for her to cling to for reassurance that he wasn't cutting her loose.

Jennifer felt her heart plummet to her toes. "Just like that?"

He nodded. "Just like that. You've got plans and dreams. You're better off without me and my baggage." His fingers closed in on her shoulder and pivoted her away from him. "Get dressed and let's get this goodbye over and done with."

This is a joke. It has to be.

Tears burned her eyes. The ache in her chest made it impossible to think straight. "You want me to forget that it happened?"

"Oh, it happened all right. You got a glimpse of the freak. Now, spare me the drama and let's go on with our separate lives."

Her mouth quivered. She thought she had broken the barrier that had divided them.

Who is this man?

She pulled on her clothes with as much dignity as she could muster. "Blake . . ."

"Jennifer, we had sex. That's all. If you are under any illusion that there is something more between us, then you are sorely mistaken," he said, and left the room.

Pride surged through her, and she straightened her back and gathered all the things she had brought with her.

She had been under the impression that things had changed between them.

The tears fell even with her best effort to hide them. Once she had cleared her things, she walked out of the room, ignoring Drew happily trailing her.

She heard dishes clanging in the kitchen, but she didn't bother to stop. He had already kicked her out of his life. There was no need to add salt to the gaping wound. Making as little noise as possible, she walked out of his house, and out of his life, just like he had ordered.

Blake stared out the window at Jennifer's retreating figure, fighting the urge to run after her and beg for forgiveness. He stayed glued to his spot and battled with the pain that had taken residence inside his chest. Moisture collected in his eyes. He hadn't cried when the RPG took everything from him, including his best friend. But as he watched her go, the impulse to cry was so strong that he caved.

What felt like a lifetime later, he collected himself and wiped the remnants of the tears from his face. He retreated to his bedroom and decided to have his way with the bottle.

I'm a grown-ass man, and I can do what I damn well please!

And alone, don't forget.

Asshole.

He found the bottle where Jennifer had left it and twisted the cap off. Taking a quick swig of the god-awful tequila, he felt the burning as the liquid slinked into his system.

"You want me to forget that it happened?"

Jennifer's question taunted him.

She just didn't understand he was doing her a big favor by letting her go. She was better off without him and his constant bouts of uncertainty. There was no them, nor would there ever be. His baggage was meant to be carried by him and only him.

Blake stripped the sheets off his bed. He couldn't endure Jennifer's lingering scent as a reminder of their night together.

Who am I kidding?

Taking one swig after another, he let his withered body collapse on the bed and kept chugging on the magical numbing extract until his mind reached the desired indifferent peak.

Several hours later, Blake awoke to the sound of hard rapping on the door and a splitting headache that doubled him over the moment he stood. He braced his hand on the wall and continued walking with his eye closed.

He yanked the door open, almost ripping the wood from its hinges. "What the hell?"

"We have to work on your people skills," Sam said, brushing past him.

"What are you doing here?" Blake slammed the door and dropped into the nearest chair, unable to keep his eye open.

"You didn't make our appointment today," Sam replied in a stern voice.

"It's not the first and it won't be the last. Don't tell me that you're doing house calls now."

"No, I'm not. I knew I was going to find you here in this pitiful state again."

Blake opened his eye and focused on Sam. "That is the reason why I don't want anyone around. I don't want your pity, her pity, or anyone else's for that matter." He felt his anger seeping out of his pores.

Sam stood towering over him with his hands clenched in tight fists by his side. "If you opened your one fuckin' good eye and smelled the friggin' roses, you would find that people don't have an ounce of pity for you. You have enough for all of us . . . *combined*."

"Then what the hell are you doing here?" Sam seemed determined to be his designated punching bag while he tried to deal with this shitty headache and all the crap surrounding Jennifer.

"Jennifer called me before she left and asked that I check on you. She guessed you'd be drowning your shit on the last thing you needed to," Sam said through clenched teeth.

Blake hadn't seen Sam lose his cool in the whole year he'd known him, but it looked as if hell was about to break loose.

Suits me just fine, big boy! Bring it.

"Jennifer and her Mother Teresa outlook rubbed off on you, my friend."

As expected, Sam grabbed him by the collar of his shirt with his big hands and dragged him outside.

Drew was hot on their heels, barking, jumping, and wanting in on the action.

"Stay, Drew," he commanded.

When they got outside, Sam released and pushed him away.

He staggered and felt as if his head might explode any second.

"C'mon, take your best shot." Sam moved into a fighting stance.

Without a word and not much planning, Blake swung a right hand in an attempted jab, followed by a left. He hit a whole lot of nothing.

Sam taunted him, gesturing for him to take another stab. "You're a lousy drunk, and an even worse friend. You've broken her heart."

"Fuck you! To hell with your charity, and I don't want her pity. I can do without those in my life." He landed a mean right hook on Sam's chin and sneered.

"You happy now?" His friend touched his jaw, looking more pissed. "You want a fight? Here I am, someone who won't take your shit."

Sam bounced up and down and bobbed side to side, and Blake struggled to keep up. When Blake took another swing, Sam blocked him and landed a punch to his gut.

Falling to his knees, Blake clutched his stomach while his wretched head continued to pound.

"This is what you wanted, right?" Sam spoke from behind.

"Yes . . ." Blake tried to get up, but the hit was pretty solid. Coupled with the alcohol that still had his head spinning, Blake knew he was beaten when he got teary-eyed and choked up with emotion. "I . . . think I messed up, my man." Sam's hand appeared in his line of vision and Blake took it.

"Sometimes, the best lessons we learn are when we're drowning." His friend helped him to his feet and dragged his sorry ass into one of the lounge chairs.

"I'm going to call things as I see them. Not going to sugarcoat it for you, brother. You're lucky to be alive, whether you believe it or not. You're not alone in that jungle you've been thrust into. But you're the only one who will dictate where you want your life to be. You've been dealt a lousy hand, but I expect that bluffer in you to mock fate and say, 'bring it.' Let the soldier in you fight 'til death, and until that last breath is taken. The fight, I think, is very much alive."

"Are you fuckin' done?" Blake asked in a hoarse voice.

"Yep. I'm good to go." Sam chuckled.

One of the things about Sam that Blake had always appreciated was that the guy didn't hold grudges.

Blake leaned on the chair and wiped the miserable tears away. Among the things that Sam said, one had shaken him to the core.

"The fight is very much alive."

The days following Jennifer's abrupt exit from Blake's life and the whirlwind move into a rented loft in LA had left her winded and bereft. Thankfully, Jennifer had been left with little time to think about him. Meetings every day for weeks to discuss projects and familiarize herself with her team of seamstresses and shoppers might have been hectic, but she was finally feeling settled both at work and home.

Jennifer had fallen into a pattern of getting up in the morning and working out at the gym, followed by showing up at work for a few hours and then continuing her work at home. Even during the weekends, she buried herself in fabrics and sketches. She had taken to phoning Mr. Smith on several occasions to water her plants and gather her mail rather than make the drive back to Lancaster. Jennifer had convinced herself it was more about getting caught up on her new job and less about getting caught by a certain nearby neighbor.

Waking up on a Sunday morning three months after she had left, Jennifer felt sluggish and decided to stay in bed for the rest of the day. It was close to supper by the time she struggled out of bed to fix a bowl of soup.

Jennifer sat in her little dining area, deep in thought, and stared at the twinkling lights of the high-rise buildings that surrounded her apartment. It dawned on her what the culprit of the lethargy and rollercoaster emotions could be, and she shook her head in denial. She rushed into the bathroom and lifted her shirt, examining her body in the mirror. Even without an apparent baby bump, the answer had been there all along. If it hadn't been for her irregular schedule, she would've suspected even sooner.

The night in the shower.

A burst of fear gripped her while she stroked her still-flat stomach. "It's going to be okay. We're going to get through this," she murmured, and patted the unnoticeable bump. She stood in the middle of the bathroom staring and let reality sink in.

For the next couple of days, Jennifer worked like a madwoman to take her mind off her discovery. Focusing her energy on her drawings, she visualized each woman wearing her creations. She concentrated on the vibrant colors, intricate embroideries, and the different designs for complementing everyone from the smallest figure to the larger.

While work made it possible to keep her mind focused on anything other than Blake, it was during the night that she lay in bed thinking about what could've been. If Blake hadn't been so stubborn, Jennifer could imagine better things between them. But at this point, she had to focus her energy on the life inside her.

Her phone rang.

"Hey! I've missed you. We need to get together soon," Coleen said, sounding as excited as ever.

"Hey, for sure. Do you want to come over?"

She had been in constant contact with Coleen. Their nightly calls helped her pass the time after dinner, when all her chores had been finished and she was left with nothing but the quiet and her thoughts. She had given Coleen a rundown of her brief relationship with Blake, but left out the part where their union created another life. It was the result of a bittersweet memory she wanted to keep to herself for a little longer.

"You have to come down this coming weekend for my baby shower."

"Oh my. Is it that time already?" With all the things that had been happening in her life, it had slipped her mind.

"Yes. Are you going to be able to get away?"

"Let me check my social calendar—" Jennifer paused for dramatic effect. "Why, yes. There is no way I'm missing your baby shower." She laughed despite the persistent sadness she often wrestled.

"Great! I'll have the guest room ready for you. I want you to stay the weekend so we have more gossip time."

With the following weekend all planned, Jennifer felt a bit better knowing she wouldn't have a chance to dwell on matters of the heart and might find the chance to break the news to her friend.

A quick call to Mr. Smith confirmed he didn't mind checking on the house and the sprinklers, and she politely listened as he caught her up on all the news. Although she missed the peace and quiet the small town offered, knowing that Blake was close by made going home a bit difficult to swallow.

"Do you want me to stop?" Jennifer asked, her voice husky, while her hand traced the scars along the side of his face and made him feel whole again.

"No." Blake moaned and shook his head. He wanted the pleasure Jennifer gave him. He inched closer until their foreheads were touching.

"I don't want to stop either. I want this . . . I want y—"

He seized her soft lips and tasted the goodness she was offering him. Her mouth was a soft fluff of clouds, and her breath was like a warm breeze. He felt her smile against his mouth, and he deepened his kiss into one that showed his need, his hunger.

With slow strokes of his tongue inside her welcoming mouth, she returned his ardent probing with fervor. He felt her shudder when she closed the gap between their bodies, tangling her legs with his. Even with their clothes on, he could feel her overheated desire that matched his own.

Blake knew where they headed, and he was okay with it. In fact, he ached for it. The inhibition was absent. The embarrassment took a leave, and all that remained was their desire to taste heaven.

Jennifer ran her fingers through his hair. "Are you sure?" she asked when their mouths broke apart. Her eyes twinkled in the soft glow coming from the lamp.

"I don't think anything can stop me now." Blake's voice dipped lower while he positioned his body on top of hers.

The mattress groaned under their collective weight when he shifted his body. He trapped her legs with his, and he let his fingers drift to the buttons of her blouse. One by one, he plucked each free. With eagerness he hadn't felt in a long time, he collected himself by taking deep breaths.

"Oh, Blake." Jennifer moaned when he pried her blouse apart to expose her breasts. Pink nipples greeted him, the perky pair he wanted to tease with his tongue and mounds he wanted to sink his face into, but instead of diving in, he captured her lips instead.

Blake was a sucker for a little foreplay even if his body was already prepping for the bigger prize. His shaft was primed to enter her now, but like a good boy he'd provide her pleasure first. Withdrawing from their kiss, he ran his lips on the side of her face and started raining kisses along her neck. He found the base of her throat and let his finger trace her collarbone where he burrowed his face into her soft skin. A jolt of pleasure swept over him.

He closed his eyes and inhaled deep, breathing her sweet scent. She moaned again, and he realized there was a real possibility that he might not last as long as he'd hoped. The woman had the power to bring him to his knees and beg for love.

Is this real?

He opened his eye and raised his head to find Jennifer smiling at him. It was real, all right.

"I'm afraid I can't wait any longer," she whispered.

Swallowing hard, Blake nodded, not trusting himself to speak for fear of ruining the moment.

Jennifer didn't waste any time in showing her eagerness. She let her hands glide to the hem of his T-shirt.

He held her hand and pointed to his face. "The scars underneath the shirt are worse."

Jennifer didn't answer, but he saw tenderness in her eyes. "I don't care what you look like. All I see is the loving guy inside and a man who makes me feel like I'm the center of his world." To prove her point, she pressed her exposed breasts on his chest, and captured his mouth for a passionate kiss. The tips of her taut nipples brushed against the material of his shirt.

He wanted nothing more than to be out of his clothes. He didn't care. Only a fool would let this woman beg. If she was willing to take him for whatever he had to offer, he wasn't going to make her wait a second longer.

Jennifer must've sensed his need. She raised his shirt and freed him from the confines of the fabric that separated them. She glanced down to his scarred body, and not once did he see her flinch.

With renewed confidence, he cupped her lush swell to taste it. While he flicked the tip of her nipple with his tongue, he let one hand play with the other breast, filling his palm like it had been made for him.

Her body undulated under his spell and her breath came in ragged spurts.

Blake lifted his face, and in the buttery glow of light, he saw the burning desire in her eyes, begging him to stop teasing and show her what he had in store for her. He slid her jeans down her legs, her dainty bikini the one thing keeping him from taking her, and he let his forefinger trace the material before he freed her body from it.

"Woman," he murmured. Her creamy skin looked like milk he could drink forever, and the gratifying prize between her legs was calling his name.

"What?" she asked, her voice demure.

"Is this what you want?" When her head bobbed several times, Blake removed his own pants before reclaiming his position on top of her.

Her body rocked upward to meet his.

"I'm not going to be gentle, Jennifer. It has been a long time—"

She placed her finger to his lips. "You can do anything that pleases you."

Sliding a hand underneath her body, he pressed his taut shaft against her belly.

Jennifer gasped and then smiled.

"You do that to me," he whispered.

"I want you now. Now . . ." She moaned and her fingers wrapped around him, stroking up and down. She caressed the tender skin around his balls until he was fully aroused. It was unhurried, deliberate, and so taking him over the edge. "I'm so wet. Please. I can't wait a second longer."

Those were the sweetest words, and ignoring the intended foreplay, he spread her legs apart and pressed himself into her welcoming body. He filled every inch of her, and her cries of pleasure made his chest puff with pride.

Blake thrust deep, testing her tight walls that wrapped around him like his very own glove. He pounded harder, loving the little moans escaping her lips.

"More . . ."

Jennifer came after a few moments. Her fulfilled cries swept across the silent room while Blake continued his vigorous thrusting.

He held his breath as he felt the release edging closer. He drove into her harder, and his body burned with lust . . . damning lust that needed release.

Blake's shouts of jubilation still echoed in his ears as he surfaced from the dream. The rude awakening felt hard and sweltering like the wildfire that was still raging inside him.

This is a fuckin' nightmare!

He jumped out of bed, ignoring the pain in his legs, and ran to the bathroom. He removed the eye patch and splashed cold water on his face, not stopping until he felt nothing.

He had let the woman go, and he deserved to be haunted by the same dreams over and over so he could dwell on the lifetime of regret for his idiocy.

"You're a fuckin' moron, Connor." Blake glared and hated the man staring back at him. The cold water on his face wasn't enough because his dick was still throbbing like hell.

Blake walked to the shower and, without bothering to remove his shorts, let the running water drown the remnant of his stunted dream.

Damn you to high heavens.

Unlike the happy-ever-after one expected from a romantic novel, his story was on its way to being a horror depiction of a man too dumb to admit that certain things happened for a reason. A dumbass too proud to accept the fact he had to fight for the love of his life.

Sam's words continued to torture him.

"The fight is very much alive."

Do I have a fight left in me . . . for Jennifer?

He knew the answer, but the first thing he had to address was his right to love her. She had given him enough reason, yet he had continued to trust his blind belief that she only felt pity. The rest had blurred along the way.

The days followed by weeks that turned into months had been terrifying. Not having her around had been the worst realization for him. Living with his scarred body was nothing compared to the reality that he'd driven Jennifer away.

Aside from his habitual drive-by, misery, self-loathing, and a bottle had been the only constants in his life. Blake still drove by Jennifer's house on a daily basis. Although he didn't expect to see her, he had taken comfort in doing what he had promised his friend in the first place.

Today, like the day before, he parked in front of her house. He pulled his cell phone out and dialed Sam. His friend was the person who'd give it to him straight up. No frills and no icing on the top.

"What's up, my man?" Sam asked.

"Meet me at Waterhole in fifteen minutes."

There was a brief silence on the phone before Sam answered. "See you there."

Exactly fifteen minutes later, the door opened and Sam stepped inside.

Once a soldier, always a soldier.

Blake was already on his second beer when Sam sat down in the booth across from him.

His first order of business was summoning the waitress for a ginger ale. "So what's up?"

"Pretty much everything," Blake answered, hating the tightness sweeping around the general area known as his heart.

Sam snorted before he brought his hands together and cracked his knuckles. He leaned forward and rested his elbows on the table and gave Blake his full attention. "Tell me about it."

"I miss her so damned much."

"And? You didn't see this one coming?"

"It seemed like the best thing to do, bro."

"Well, I knew it was just a matter of time 'til you realized you acted like an ass."

"I know." It was tough to admit that he had screwed up so thoroughly. But he was an unemployed veteran who was disfigured inside as well as out.

"So why am I here? To tell you what you already know?" Sam drummed his fingers on the table.

Blake pounded his fist in response, rattling the bottles and spilling some of the beer on the table. "Fine, I guess I screwed up big time. But why can't I get her out of my mind?"

His lamentation was met with sympathetic eyes. "Let me ask you this. What do you intend to do for the rest of your life? And don't lie to me, because I know you well enough."

The waitress approached their table with Sam's drink.

Blake waited for her to walk away before he answered. "I don't know. I guess continue living. Find a job somewhere."

The future sounded bleak without a concrete plan, but it was all he had. He took a swig of his beer and watched as the bubbles settled inside the bottle.

"Do you see Jennifer in your future at all?" Sam took a long sip from his glass.

"What kind of a question is that?"

His friend chuckled. "Just answer it."

"Sometimes . . ."

"If you could have her back in your life, would it make a difference?"

Blake stared at Sam and had no idea how to answer, especially since he had avoided the thought. Or maybe it was the fear of hope.

"Of course it would, but look at me. I'm full of self-doubt, I look like a drunken sailor all the time, and I'm fuckin' hideous."

"Would you, for one second, admit that you'll do whatever it takes to get her back?" Sam took another long pull on his ale, downing half its contents in a single gulp.

"I guess I will . . . but I'm so fucked up. Why would she want me?" he asked.

"You're still fucked up." Sam laughed, adding to Blake's annoyance. "Here's what I think you can do. Get out of the hole you dug for yourself and stop dwelling on the things you can't change. Call your superior officer and ask for a desk job, or anything that would put you back in the workforce. Then, see a shrink. I doubt I'm much help to you." Sam winked. "Attend your therapies and try to smile a bit more. You're not carrying the weight of the world, you know."

"As easy as that?" He wished things were as simple as his friend made it sound.

"No. It won't be easy. First, get that damn chip off your shoulder and take all the help you can get. Next, understand it's going to take a lot of perseverance and patience on your part, but it can be done. I have faith in you."

"What if I fall flat on my face?" Blake could barely swallow around the lump in his throat, but if he was going to start anywhere, he may as well start with his worst fear.

"Stop screwing around. Go get her if you want her, instead of hiding inside your house like a hermit waiting for Armageddon."

"Screw you." Although Sam was right, he hated hearing it.

"Sure, Blake, go right ahead. Don't you think I don't feel your pain, bro? We've been together for a long time, and I know you as well as I know my dick."

Blake grimaced at the mental picture while Sam smiled.

"Stop being a pussy and pursue the woman. If she is the one who can ring your bell, just do us all a favor and snap out of that asshole act."

"You make it sound so easy. What if it doesn't work out?"

"The ball's in your court. It's time to go out and play." Sam looked pretty pleased with himself.

"I don't think I can handle a rejection." Blake sighed.

"If she rejects you, you're better off than where you are now. It's better than not trying at all. When you're all straightened out, let me know and I'll tell you where to find her."

Blake left the bar after two beers, with a whole new perspective. The talk with Sam had given him a direction that had been too blurry for him to see at first, but with his friend showing the map and a few coordinates, he knew what he had to do. If he could break away from the uncertainties that plagued him, it wouldn't be difficult. He simply had to look at this with an open mind—as a challenge— to better himself and reach a level where he could offer himself to the woman he loved. There were many things he needed to do and one person to talk to so he could start clearing the air once and for all.

Baby steps.

When Blake turned onto his street, he noticed a black Crown Victoria parked in front of his house. As he rolled closer, he saw the official government license plate and his heart skipped.

He parked and jumped out, feeling light on his feet. It looked like one of his baby steps might have come to him instead.

The familiar face of Colonel Norwalk greeted him as Blake approached the front door. Blake stopped short, snapping into the familiar and surprisingly comfortable greeting. "Sir!"

Colonel Norwalk returned the salute and gave him a broad smile. "Connor, it's been a while. How have you been?" The man who had been like a father during his military career regarded him with probing pale blue eyes, and Blake felt something coming.

"I'm fine, sir." He opened the front door, and Drew came scuttling out to greet him and then approached his visitor with caution. "Easy, boy," he said to the dog, and then turned to the colonel. "Make yourself comfortable while I let this one out."

He led Drew to the back and opened the slider then returned. "This is a pleasant surprise, sir. What can I do for you?"

Colonel Norwalk was lounging comfortably with his legs crossed when Blake walked in. He uncrossed them and leaned forward as Blake sat down. "We're not active, so please, call me Lance."

It felt awkward to call someone he'd respected all his service life by his first name, but this sounded like an order, so he nodded.

"I'm here on official and unofficial business. Let me start with the unofficial." Lance produced a legal-sized white envelope from the breast pocket of his uniform and handed it to him.

"What is this?" Blake took the envelope, noticed his name on it, and immediately recognized Trent's penmanship.

"It was among the things sent to Trent's parents. It landed on my desk last week. Since I was paying you a visit, I decided to bring it with me." Lance leaned back and seemed to be giving Blake a moment to check the contents first.

He placed the envelope on the coffee table and looked up. "I think I'm ready for the official business."

"All right. I'm here to offer you a job. Again . . ."

Blake stared at the older man, stunned and unable to form a coherent answer. Just when he thought he'd lost his chance. He coughed and then cleared his throat. "A job?"

"I received word that you have taken steps to rejoin the living." Lance laughed.

"What do you mean?"

"I keep tabs on my men. I want to see which among them, after life-altering changes, would bounce back fast. I heard from your eye doctor and received the full report from Sam Sweeney."

Blake clenched his jaw and held his breath as his head spun out of control with all the what ifs.

"The job deals with training new recruits. I'll give you six months to get back in shape. When I say shape, I mean tip-top, and I want you tight up here." Lance pointed to his temple. "After that, I want you to report for briefing before you're given the exact nature of your assignment."

Unable to believe what he was hearing, Blake remained silent while he tried to digest the information. This was the first step he needed to take charge, instead of playing victim all the time.

"This doesn't put you on active duty, considering the beating you received out there, but it's just as good as. Unless you wanted a desk job instead?" The man waggled his bushy eyebrows.

"No, sir," he replied. In truth, this went beyond anything he'd expected after all that had happened. He had been longing for the familiar scent of exhilaration, the prospect of planning, and an active role in getting things done.

Lance's eyes softened. "Is that a yes?"

Blake nodded several times, not trusting himself to say the words right away. His eyes began to moisten and that was the last thing he wanted his superior to see.

Lance stood up and walked over to place a hand on Blake's shoulder. "Then we got ourselves a deal. Remember, six months. No more, no less. I want you to show the eager boys what we're all about."

Blake stood up and offered his hand. "Thank you for the opportunity to serve again." His voice was raw with emotions he couldn't seem to control.

"No thanks necessary." The colonel shook his hand. "I'll stay in touch."

After Lance had left, Blake hurried to let Drew in. "Good news, boy. It looks like I have a job again."

Drew wagged his tail as if he understood Blake's happiness.

He patted the dog's head and gave him his favorite pig ear treat, then he returned to the living room.

Not knowing what to expect, he opened the envelope and unfolded the letter on the familiar yellow-lined notepaper that his friend had used whenever he wrote his letters to Jennifer.

December 10, 2001

Bro,

I have no idea why I'm writing this, but I've had a bad feeling lately. I hate to sound morbid, but it feels like something's coming, and I want to take this time to clear the air between us concerning the last conversation we had about Jennifer.

I'm scared I won't make her happy because I can't be the husband I wanted to be. Hell, I know I'm wussing out. I see it happening, but it'll only get worse if I marry her. My Jennifer would understand, I know that, because she's compassionate and tenderhearted, but I couldn't live with myself. So I'm cutting my losses now.

You may not understand it, but I hope you will in time. It's like that old saying—the one about loving someone so much that you let them go. If it's meant to be, they come back. If not . . .

You're not the only sensitive one on the team, bud. I sit and observe, too, and as your brother, I know what's in your heart, even if you refuse to admit it.

I know how you feel about Jennifer. How you really feel. And I want you to be happy just as much as I do her. No one deserves her love more than you. Cherish her, brother, like she should be cherished.

I need you to know I'm okay with this, Blake, whatever happens. I know it's right, and you are right for her.

Take good care of each other.

Trent

Fighting tears made it difficult to breathe as he stared at the letter Trent had written two days before he died. Blake wasn't one to believe in omens, sixth sense, signs, and all that bullshit, but the timing of all this made the hair on the back of his neck rise.

He read the letter once more before tucking it safely away. Today, everything had fallen into place. One opportunity after another had arrived on his doorstep, and he'd be an idiot not to grab hold of every chance he had and to go after the woman who completed him.

—⁓—

Blake sat in the posh reception area of one of the best real estate agents he knew. He looked around the luxurious office while several people walked in and out, surreptitiously giving him a curious glance. He smoothed his white long-sleeve shirt and closed his eyes. At Sam's insistence, he had shed the beanie that had become his security blanket from the prying stares.

The new Blake was taking a lot of getting used to, but he wasn't complaining. This was part of the process. Getting better was the goal. This appointment was made to serve two purposes, and he couldn't wait to take care of this unfinished business.

"Mr. Connor?"

He looked up at the receptionist and nodded.

"Ms. Hill is ready for you."

He stood up and followed the woman into a hallway lined with plush beige carpeting until they reached a mahogany door at the end.

She tapped the door before opening it.

The woman behind the desk was just as he remembered her—beautiful, sharp-looking, with vibrant blue eyes. Time had been kind to her.

"Blake," she said, after the receptionist had left. "It's been a while."

"Yes . . ." He sat down on the chair she gestured at and made himself comfortable.

"You look different." Her surprised reaction wasn't unexpected. Katrina had seen him at his worst.

Not used to the attention, he raked his hand through his hair. "It's the new and improved Blake, I guess."

She smiled before getting down to business. "To what do I owe this surprise visit?"

"Katrina, I want to apologize for the way things ended between us. I—"

"You saved us from making a big mistake."

He watched her for any hint of resentment, or even anger, but he found none.

She returned his gaze and shrugged. "True, I was hurt in the beginning, and I tried to get back at you by going out with Dwight. But, looking back on it, it was meant to be. I'm happily married."

Relief washed over him. "But you're still using your maiden name?"

"Familiarity is important in this field. Clients are used to my name, so Dwight and I decided it was best to keep it." She twirled a strand of hair around her finger just like she had done so many times in the past.

"Well, I'm glad you're happy."

"And you? How are you?"

He gave her a wistful smile. "I'm all right." He rested his arms on the desk in an effort to keep from wringing his hands together.

She smiled. "I'm sure you can do better than that."

He took a deep breath, hating to sound like the pathetic soul that he was. "I'm in love with this woman."

"It's Trent's girl, isn't it?" There was no malice in Katrina's tone, just an honest-to-goodness question that deserved a straight answer.

"Yes."

"I've always known, but you never had the courage to admit it to yourself."

"You knew all along?"

Katrina nodded. "I knew I was fooling myself that you would learn to love me back." She rolled her eyes and changed the subject. "We've known each other long enough for me to recognize that look. What's troubling you?"

"I want you to help me find something. This is my silly attempt at being romantic."

Katrina leaned forward and placed a hand on top of his. "I'm all ears."

One month later . . .

Jennifer said a quick goodbye to Coleen and her husband. She got in her car and headed north for the two-hour drive back to LA. It had been a magical weekend filled with family love, warmth, and laughter. Although Coleen tried her best to include Jennifer by filling her in on private jokes and gossip, she had still felt like an outsider. Seeing Coleen's bond with John and their family and friends made her heart ache at the thought of not having it all as well, of her child growing up without a father.

Jennifer shook her head, dispelling the melancholy, and concentrated on the road. The drive was pleasant from San Diego County, with fewer cars than usual clogging up the interstate.

As she drew closer to the city, the glittering skyscrapers loomed ahead. The life in the city had its ups and downs. Still a small town girl at heart, the snarling traffic and busy noise of the downtown area had proven to be problematic and overwhelming. The good thing about living in a busy metropolis was the proximity to restaurants and all other establishments. It didn't hurt that she felt safe and comfortable in her loft, which was a relief considering her work hours were as unpredictable as the weather.

She had enjoyed the weekend away but she was ready for her time alone. Flicking the garage door opener, she waited until it was clear to proceed. She took the winding trail of pavement to the tenth level and slammed on her brakes.

Jennifer held her breath upon seeing a familiar brown Jeep parked in the space next to her designated spot. Easing off the brake pedal and into her assigned space, she watched as a figure emerged from the vehicle. Her heart pounded against her chest, and she found it impossible to think.

She might not have recognized Blake if not for the familiar smirk as he leaned against his Jeep, arms crossed, and watching her like a hawk.

She gripped the steering wheel, vacillating between backing out of the parking deck and staying.

Well, at least he can't throw me out of my own place.

Jennifer braced her shoulders and took deep calming breaths.

How had he known where she lived and the time she was coming back? The answer to the former had to be Sam. Jennifer needed to have a word with him at her soonest convenience.

She slid out of her compact car, ready for a war of words.

Blake raked his eyes over her figure, his brows furrowing.

If he could stand there and study her like a science experiment, she could do the same.

She took her sweet time assessing the man who haunted her dreams.

What's different? He is not wearing his beanie and—oh my God. His new eye!

"Where have you been? Don't you know people are worried about you?" he asked in the usual authoritative tone he'd used so often.

Jennifer smiled sweetly as though his presence had no effect on her. She smoothed her white linen pants and her ivory blouse that showed her suntanned skin. She knew she looked good, even if her heart was ramming harder against her ribs with each passing second. "I don't answer to anyone."

Blake scowled and she walked past him to the loft entrance.

She heard his footsteps as he trailed after her.

"Aren't you even going to say hello?" he asked.

She threw a glare at him over her shoulder and noticed his hair was cut in a neat style that showed his face and the scars. "Not if you're going to talk to me that way." She kept walking. When she reached her door, she stopped and turned around. "I invite friends in but you don't fit the category."

She watched as Blake's eyebrows lifted and his lips thinned then he exhaled. "Hello, Jennifer Owens. I'm Blake Connor. It's nice to meet you. Where the hell have you been?"

Jennifer shook her head and decided to push back. "What's it to you?" She turned and inserted the key with fumbling fingers, hating Blake's effect on her.

Damn it, door! Open . . . now!

The door finally cooperated and she opened it just enough to let herself in, but Blake wedged his foot against it, preventing her from closing it in his face.

"It would have been nice if you let someone know."

That does it!

She huffed, let go of the door, and stomped into the living room. "Who should I call? In case you missed the memo, everyone I know is dead!" She threw her purse on the coffee table and marched straight to the big picture window, hoping the city landscape would calm her nerves.

"You could have called me. I was worried about you. I've been camped in my Jeep the entire weekend. If not for your nice neighbor, I would have been waiting out on the street."

"You don't have to worry about me." She turned in time to catch him walking toward her, his gait predatory, but his expression had remarkably softened.

"But I am worried about you."

Oh, no, not the charm. No, sir.

She took a step back, then another and another, until her back hit the window. "You could've fooled me. You're just upset because you don't have anyone to order around."

Blake stopped in front of her and placed his hands inside his jeans pockets. "I've said a lot of foolish and hurtful things. I can't take them away, but I didn't mean any of 'em. I'm here because I want to beg forgiveness."

Jennifer opened her mouth, ready to sling a retort, but closed it again.

Apologize?

She studied him for a moment, gauging his mood. She saw the subtle and not-so-subtle changes in him—the lighter movement, the absent scathing tone, and his improved overall appearance.

Can it be?

She shook her head. "And then what?" She slid past him.

Blake turned around. "And then, *if* forgiven, I want to make love with you, without the fear and self-loathing this time."

Her mouth gaped open and blood rushed to her face. She'd heard him say a lot of crazy things in the past, but this one topped the bill.

What an arrogant prick!

She threw her hands up and began to pace. "You are the most obnoxious person I've ever met!"

"And yet, you love me for all my faults, don't you?"

Jennifer stopped and closed her eyes. She wanted to tell him that he meant nothing, but she couldn't bring herself to do it. Jutting her chin, she gritted her teeth and nodded. "I do, but that's beside the point. You're not right up there." She pointed to his head. "You turn away those who love you, and I'm afraid that I'll end up hating you if I don't stay out of your life."

Blake took several steps forward, reaching for her.

She shook her head.

"After you left, my world was turned upside down. It took a good beating to get where I am now."

She met his gaze straight on. "Exactly where are you, Blake Connor?"

"I'm where I have to be. This may come as a shock to you but I'm happy in my own skin, whatever it looks like, and I'm ready to think of the future." He gave her a small smile, and despite her resolve not crumbling, her heart was thawing.

"What is the future for you?" Her voice dipped lower, thinking of the baby inside her.

"I see you in it," he said in a husky voice.

When he reached for her hand, she allowed him to hold her. His hand was rough, but warm to touch and very, very familiar. "Why are you doing this to me?"

Blake drew her closer and she let him. He placed one hand on the small of her back and Jennifer rested her head on his chest.

She breathed in his masculine scent, the familiar one that never failed to make her all tingly.

"Because I'm in love with you, Jennifer Owens. I've loved you from the moment Trent first showed me your picture. I loved you every day I drove past your house in Lancaster, and I want to love you for the rest of my life."

She heard the rapid beating of his heart and she ached to believe him. He made it sound so enticing. Would she dare give her heart and risk getting hurt again?

"I want you in my bed. I want to call you my wife, and I would love to show you what the new and improved me is all about . . . if you'll have me."

Jennifer hesitated.

Tell him.

How?

What if he doesn't believe me?

She pushed him back to get a better look at his face. "I'm not built for this free-falling relationship. I don't even know you. All I remember is the man who kept pushing me away. A bitter person who despised life because he'd been dealt a bad hand. You refused to see that I love the man and everything about him. How do you expect me to just believe in what you're saying now?"

Instead of answering her, he captured her mouth in a rough and demanding kiss.

Her heart started beating wildly as the memories of his touch flooded her, making her remember their nights together. Sweet tingles of apprehension surged through her veins. When he stopped to look at her, her mouth prickled from his punishing kisses.

"I will make you believe it every day of my life. I'm not asking you to make a decision now. All I'm asking you for is the chance to make you happy." One hand trailed up and down her arm in a caress.

"I don't know what to say. I have so many questions."

"I'll be happy to answer them inside your bedroom." He breathed against her cheek, lifting her into his arms and carrying her up the steps.

Heat coursed through her, and no matter how much she wanted to deny him, her body had been pining for him for so long. She doubted she would last any longer under the intense pressure of his presence and his words.

When Blake laid her down, she pulled him on top of her. His eye sparked a deep flame of desire she knew was flashing in her own. He seized her mouth for a long kiss. This time it was unhurried, as if he had all the time in the world. Then he worked his mouth down to her chin, placing small kisses on her neck and throat.

Jennifer smiled, loving the buildup, for she knew it wouldn't take Blake long before he tasted her. She teemed with excitement when he sat up, his legs cradling her, and began unbuttoning her blouse.

"I love the feel of this fabric." He was breathing hard, and she knew that he was feeling the heat just like she did.

"It's silk." Having him so close to her made it impossible to think clearly. Jennifer closed her eyes for a brief moment and let out a moan as the last button came undone.

"I could look at your . . ." Blake's eyes grew wide. He looked at her then back to her stomach. "Are you—is it mine?"

Jennifer nodded and ran her palm over her growing belly. "I'm going on four months."

"How? When? I was protected the last time we . . ." There was no denial in his tone, just bewilderment. "Did it happen the night I was . . ."

She closed her eyes again, feeling the guilt of keeping an important detail from him for a long time. "The night when you were drunk. You wanted to shower. I wouldn't leave you alone for fear that you might hurt yourself. And then it happened." Jennifer opened her eyes to find Blake staring at her, his eye misting.

"I'm not turning my back on my responsibility. This baby will have my name." Blake kissed her stomach before inching up to capture her mouth.

Overwhelmed by his words and the sudden turn of events, Jennifer responded with eager kisses then it dawned on her what he'd said. "Is that what I am to you? A responsibility you have to shoulder? Because I can make it on my own. You don't have to feel obligated—"

"You haven't listened to a word I've said. I wanted to marry you even before I found out you were pregnant. But now . . . there is no way I'll let my child be born without my name and knowing how much his father loves him."

"You think it's a boy?"

He smiled. "It's going to be a boy. I can feel it."

"I don't know what to say. I want—"

"What I want right now is to feel your body against mine."

Fiery heat emboldened her. Jennifer relieved him of his shirt with frantic fingers while she marveled at the changes in him. He didn't flinch when her gaze travelled to his chest, along his strong stomach and each scar that defined him as the man she had fallen in love with. She longed to feel his hard muscles brushing against the softness of her skin. Her gaze ended at the button of his jeans. The hair peeking from the waistband taunted her to unfasten the darn button, the one obstacle that was keeping her from fully appreciating his body.

She sat up and planted a kiss on his parted lips once she got her fill. Tilting her head, she let her finger trace the softness of his lips.

He used his tongue to suck her finger inside, circling, eliciting an involuntary shudder from her.

As her finger kept him busy, she caressed his back with her other palm, tracing the flexed muscles and feeling each ripple with every movement.

"You're a tease," he said when her finger slid out. Without a word, he reached around her back and released the bra that held her breasts prisoner. He let his eyes wander, grinning as they devoured all she had to offer. He reached out, gathered one nipple between his thumb and forefinger, and pinched.

She moaned at the delicious sensation shooting from the perky tip.

"Blake, I love and hate foreplay," she complained.

"I'm afraid we've entered the no stopping zone," he said, before his mouth descended on one of her sensitive mounds. Blake let his tongue glide across her skin, up and down the sloping playground, lapping, teasing, and making her wish for heaven right that moment.

"I won't let you stop."

He continued his assault on her breasts, keeping his tongue rigid while he flicked repeatedly on her nipple, punishing her with pleasure and urging her to scream.

She released a loud sigh of contentment while her fingers raked through the silky strands of his hair.

Blake pleasured each breast until her toes curled and her bud throbbed with want. Arching her body with each of his punishing demands, she met his touches with pained pleasure.

He grazed his hand down her abdomen, stopping to rub her belly before moving down to her pants.

Jennifer bucked her hips upward, eager to meet his touch.

He spread the zipper apart, and a flame ignited within her.

Jennifer wished he could douse her fire soon, but she loved the anticipation enough to stay patient.

He peeled her slacks off, taking her thong in the process with one powerful sweep, and her skin burned even hotter. He nudged her down and spread himself on top of her.

Blake lifted her and cupped her bottom, running his hands along her overheated skin that was screaming for more. The friction of his calloused palm against her skin stirred more desire, and her lips parted. Sliding his tongue in between her lips, he teased her to action, and she sucked hard and unrelenting.

She roamed her hands over the button of his pants that separated her from ecstasy. She looked up at him, sensing his hesitation, but there was no stopping her now. "Are you okay with this?"

Please say yes.

When he nodded and his breathing relaxed, she released the fly and his erection greeted her. She swayed at the electrifying sight before her.

Blake moved fast to get rid of his pants and was soon as naked as she was. Remembering how self-conscious he had been their first time, the man before her barely resembled the old one.

Blake let her memorize every bit of him, from the thin strip of hair that trailed from below his belly button and running down to his curls. She gazed at the scarring that ran down his leg, loving every second of watching every bit of his body. Taking his proud erection in her palm, she gave it a little action, stroking gently. He groaned his contentment, grinding his hips with her every thrust. She was damp and so ready to take it a step further.

After several hard thrusts against her palm, he withdrew from her grasp. "I brought protection, but I see no point in using it now." His voice was thick with emotions. "Am I going to hurt the baby?"

"No," she whispered.

Like a bolt of lightning, Blake sheathed himself in her.

She cried at the sweet intrusion when he pulled out and plunged back in. He repeated the process until her head was about to explode, with no coherent thoughts but the fulfillment she was aching for. She hit her climax and burst into a mind-numbing rapture. "Oh, Blake." Her cries shattered with her.

Blake followed, arching his back, shuddering and exploded to his peak. "Oh, baby, baby!" He kept shouting until the last of his pleasure ebbed and he collapsed next to her.

How she ended in heaven when she thought her life would wither away might have had her questioning her luck before, but she wasn't going to ask anymore. She would never forget the sweetness of this moment.

Blake hoisted his body on his elbows while watching Jennifer walk to the bathroom. He heard the running water and closed his eyes. Still reveling in the aftermath of their sweet reunion, he let the glorious thoughts warm him.

During the night, as Jennifer had slept, Blake watched her and kept thanking his lucky stars for paving a way back into her life. And the biggest surprise of all, she was having his baby. He was never going to let them go.

Jennifer came out in her robe, her face freshly scrubbed, and the glow of their lovemaking radiating on her face. She smiled when their eyes met, and descended the stairs to the main part of the loft.

She fascinated him. Her little smile showed strength underneath the layer of sweetness, and most of all, he loved her courage for giving him another chance.

Did she?

Rewinding every bit of their conversation from last night, she hadn't said that he was back in her life. Sure, she had accepted his explanations, but there had been no mention of anything more. She wanted to talk. She had said so last night.

Taking a deep breath, Blake rose from the bed and picked up his discarded jeans. He made his way downstairs and found Jennifer by the window, staring off into the distance, a cup of coffee in hand. The view of the sleepy city with a few twinkling lights pulsing in every direction was something he could get used to.

He stopped behind her and placed both palms on her shoulders. "Good morning," he said, and lowered his face on her neck, skimming his mouth on her soft skin.

She sighed and tilted her head to the side.

He ravaged the silky expanse with kisses until he wanted more. Though he'd had wicked dreams of making love with her on every surface of the loft, he knew they should talk first.

Jennifer turned around, her eyes glistening with tears. "You know I love you, right?" Her voice broke.

Blake frowned, searching her face for a trace of the happiness he thought he'd seen the night before. "Jennifer, I love you, more than myself," he whispered, hating himself for feeling so vulnerable. He curbed his impulse to clam up and hide. Showing her his weaknesses was an integral part of his road to fully accepting himself, as well as his faults.

"I'm scared," she said, placing one hand on his chest.

He felt her emotions through her touch and the way her body vibrated. He nodded. "I'm scared, too," he murmured into her hair.

"What's going to happen to us and the baby? I can't handle your highs and lows. I already know that."

After many visits with the shrink, he had been prepped to face her doubts about him. Although he didn't have the concrete answers, he knew what he could to do to keep himself together and put her worries to rest.

"I don't expect you to fully trust me after the way I've treated you. All I can promise you is honesty. I pledge to keep you close when fears and insecurities get the best of me. I won't shut you out. It's going to be a work in progress, but I assure you that through all of it, I will try to protect you . . . even from me and my mood swings. I will guard our child from all things that would hurt him, and be the best father I can be. I will love him with everything I have."

She gazed up at him. "I don't need you to protect me. I want to feel everything you feel. Don't shield me from the horrors of your experience.

All I ask is to allow me to be a part of all that you are . . .”

"I want you to be happy with me. Heaven knows, I hated seeing you unhappy. I wanted to shoot myself every time I lashed out at you. I was foolish to think I ever saw pity in your eyes. I believed the worst because I thought I was protecting myself." He took the mug from her and placed it on the glass table, and then he took her hand and led her to the sofa. Patting his thigh, he waited for her to come to him.

She sat on his lap, still seeming uncertain what to say while she trailed her fingers along the scar on his face.

Blake closed his eyes, savoring the caress and letting her touch fill him with courage. "I don't expect you to believe what I say now. All I can ask is for you to stay by me while I figure things out."

A small smile tugged at the corner of her lips and she watched him with tenderness that he welcomed. "I think I can do that," she said. "I'm going to be by your side supporting and loving you."

"I have no idea what I did to deserve your love, but I'm grateful for a chance to make you happy." He touched her face and traced his finger over her soft lips.

She sighed. "How do you propose on starting this happy plan? My work won't allow me to be anywhere else at the moment. I know you have your therapy and such, and I wouldn't ask you to give it up."

"I have access to a good therapist anywhere, although I'm going to miss Sam's hardcore approach. I'm not asking you to give up anything for me either. In fact, I'm going to start work in a few months."

She threw her hands around his neck and pulled him close for a congratulatory kiss.

Heat radiated throughout his body by the time their sweet kiss ended.

"I'm so happy for you." Her eyes started misting.

"Are you okay with the prospect of being an army wife and raising an army brat?" He watched the blood drain from her face, and he held his breath.

She didn't say a word but her smile said everything he needed to hear.

He sighed in relief.

She wiggled on his lap, snuggling closer, and froze. "Is this what I think it is?" she asked in a tiny voice, sounding hopeful.

He nodded and placed her on the sofa. He fished inside his jeans pocket for the gift he had wanted to give her last night. Dropping to his knees, he smiled up at her while he presented her with a purple velvet box. Her mouth gaped when he revealed a ring with a heart-shaped diamond. "Will you share my life as my wife, through happiness and tears, and all my highs and lows?"

"Yes. I will be your wife and whatever you need me to be." She lowered her mouth to his for a brief kiss while he slipped the ring on her finger.

"Thank you for taking the chance with me."

"I love you, Blake. I want to be with you forever."

"Forever."

She gazed down at her ring finger. "This is beautiful."

"It fits my beautiful bride-to-be." He beamed. "Mom helped me picked it out."

Happiness shone in her tender smile. She fell on her knees and took his hands in hers. "I hope I can make you as happy as you have made me."

"Agreeing to be my wife is the first step, my girl." He brought her hands to his lips and kissed them, then he pulled her to her feet and snaked his arms around her waist.

Her smile faded. "You're not going back into active duty, are you?"

"No. My combat days are over. I will be working and might be away from time to time, but I will always be a phone call away. I'm going to train eager souls from now on." He smiled, touched at her concern.

"Will you be able to pursue your other dream, too?" she asked, sounding tentative.

He frowned, not sure what she meant. "What other dream?"

"Writing music, playing . . ."

"I have enough time for that, along with raising little ones with you in *our* house just a few minutes away from this crazy city."

"You bought a house?" she asked.

He chuckled. "I happen to have a good friend that happens to be a great real estate agent. Katrina found us a perfect house. In hindsight, I probably should have gotten your yes first, but I'm glad I went for it. It's obvious that someone up there wanted our baby to have a home to come home to."

"I like that."

"If you have time today, I want us to visit someone special."

"I've got all the time in the world for you, Blake Connor. I agreed to forever, remember?"

His chest swelled with happiness. He pulled her into his arms and held her for a long time.

A few hours later . . .

"Hey, bud," Blake whispered to the vast blue sea surrounding them.

At Trent's request, his ashes had been sprinkled in the ocean by his parents. This was the one place Blake knew he could reach his friend.

He invited Jennifer to join him at the end of the boardwalk by the pier.

She gathered her skirt and sat next to him.

The rays of the morning sun cast a shimmering glow as they kissed the water, lending a serene backdrop amid the crying of the seagulls.

He inhaled deep and let out a contented sigh. "You called it right. I am in love with our girl. In fact, I'm making her my wife."

Jennifer squeezed his hand.

He glanced at her and smiled before returning his gaze to the expanse of water before him, and paid homage to his best friend.

Your secret's safe, brother, and as promised I will keep watch over her. Her happiness will be my life's purpose. I love you, Trent. Stay tight.

He placed his fist over his heart and vowed to never forget the man he had not only called a friend but his brother-in-arms.

Acknowledgement

Thank you very much to these wonderful gals, who kept me sane and motivated—Wendy Depperschmidt, Kristen Giles, Claudia Trapp, Judith Somera, Mavvy Vasquez, Lucia Morales, and Donna Rogers.

Trenda Lundin—I owe you another trip to the beach and In-N-Out Burger for encouraging me to complete this project. I'm deeply grateful for your constant reminders that I was onto something good. This story is as much yours as it is mine. I'm ready to share Blake.

DJ Gann—thank you for your patience and guidance during the entire editing process.

With love to my family.

And to all the men and women who are currently serving or have served in the military—your service, dedication, and sacrifice are appreciated.

About the Author

A professional daydreamer, Lorenz Font discovered her love of writing after reading a celebrated novel that inspired one idea after another. Since being published in 2013, she has been conspiring, butting heads, and enjoying her spare time with vampires, angels, samurais, and other creatures she has created in her head.

Her perfect day consists of writing and lounging on her garage couch (a.k.a. the office) with a glass of her favorite cabernet while listening to her ever-growing music collection. She finds writing urban fantasy exhilarating and places an intense focus on angst and the redemption of flawed characters. Her fascination with romantic twists is a mainstay in all her stories.

Lorenz lives in Southern California with her supportive family and three demanding dogs. divides her time between a full-time job and her busy writing schedule.